MW00638292

HER TEMPTING PROTECTOR

NIGHT STORM, BOOK TWO

CAITLYN O'LEARY

© Copyright 2020 Caitlyn O'Leary
All rights reserved.
All cover art and logo © Copyright 2020
By Passionately Kind Publishing Inc.
Cover by Lori Jackson Design
Edited by Rebecca Hodgkins
Content Edited by Trenda Lundin
Cover Photo by Wander Aguiar Photography

All rights reserved. No part of this book may be reproduced in any form or by any electronic or mechanical means, including information storage and retrieval systems—except in the case of brief quotations embodied in critical articles or reviews—without permission in writing from the author.

This book is a work of fiction. The names, characters, and places portrayed in this book are entirely products of the author's imagination or used fictitiously. Any resemblance to actual events, locales or persons, living or dead, is entirely coincidental and not intended by the author.

The unauthorized reproduction or distribution of this copyrighted work is illegal. Criminal copyright infringement, including infringement without monetary gain, is investigated by the FBI and is punishable by up to five years in federal prison and a fine of $250,000.

If you find any eBooks being sold or shared illegally, please contact the author at Caitlyn@CaitlynOLeary.com.

To my husband John, who always tempts me while still having my back.

SYNOPSIS

CAN HE GET THEM TO SAFETY IN TIME?

Navy SEAL, Cullen Lyons, knew the moment he saw Dr. Carys Adams treating her patients in an African war zone that she was stubborn, selfless and extraordinary. Ignoring the danger surrounding her, she concentrated on keeping the young mother and newborn alive. Now it was Cullen's job to evade the brutal rebel forces who had targeted Carys and the young family and get them to safety.

HOW WILL THEY SURVIVE?

Carys knows that a three day journey to Khartoum could kill her patients, but staying in hiding would sign their death warrant. She had never met a man like Cullen Lyons, every instinct told her that she could trust him, that she had finally found someone she could lean on, but what if she was wrong? Was he really the hero he seemed to be?

"*D*oc, is it as bad as I think it is?"

Dr. Carys Adams glanced sideways at the sweating man who had been assigned to lead their security detail here in Sudan.

Had he really just asked that?

Carys glanced back out the window, it felt like there were at least forty gun barrels pointed directly at her head. There weren't, it just seemed like it. Logically she knew they were trying to protect the hospital from the Rapid Support Force troops who had been responsible for the massacre last summer, but that still didn't make it any easier for her to see all the matte black steel in the crowd. She swallowed down bile-flavored saliva, then tried to calm her expression before turning back to Hans.

"It's bad, really bad. Hans, I need you to do me a favor."

"Anything," he nodded.

"Get Isaac down here, then you go back and make

sure all of the nurses have the patients ready to evacuate. I don't want one single patient left behind. Do a double sweep, make sure you don't miss anyone."

"Why do you need Isaac?" His voice was petulant.

Oh, for pity's sake, was he worried that she was giving Isaac a more important job when they were about to be killed? Or worse? Again, her thoughts went back to what had happened here in Khartoum a few months back before the regime change.

She rested her hand on Han's forearm. "I know I can depend on you to keep those people safe. I can, can't I?" she asked softly. He stood straighter.

"I won't let you down, Dr. Adams."

Great, he responded to flattery, instead of just getting the job done like he should.

He started to sprint across the dilapidated linoleum lobby. Then he turned back when he hit the elevator button. "I'll make sure the patients stay safe," he promised.

"Hans, the power's iffy. Take the stairs just to be safe." She kept her voice low, but loud enough to carry across the empty room. She gritted her teeth at his ineptitude.

He ran to the stair entrance.

Carys went back to looking out the window through the blinds. With the angle of the sun, nobody could see through her vantage point. She watched as a beautiful woman in a bright orange robe spoke from the back of a truck. She had a bullhorn in one hand, and her other hand pointed upwards to heaven. She spoke Arabic to the crowd, telling them that their new prime minister was their way to salvation. He would save them from their decades of struggles. He was their nation's salvation.

Carys hoped she was right. She hadn't just bet her life on the new prime minister, she had bet her team's lives on the regime change.

The woman continued. Abdalla Hamdok was a man to believe in. Her voice was melodic as she explained that he was a steadfast man with a realistic vision for his nation. Carys concurred.

When his people had contacted her two months ago to consult with the Central Committee of Sundanese Doctors, she'd weighed all the pros and cons, and finally agreed to take the assignment in Sudan. Especially knowing that she would be reunited with one of her med-school friends, Joyce Dandekar, who'd been a surgeon at the hospital in Sudan's capital city of Khartoum, a huge modern city of five million. It had a deadly regime change, but that was over—she'd been so sure.

But here she was, once again in the middle of a bad dream.

Please, God, don't let it turn into something like the horror she'd lived through almost four years ago in Santa Flores.

Carys heard the stair door open and turned to see Isaac move quickly and gracefully toward her, he was tall and thin, with a commanding presence. As he got to her, he gently pulled her to the side of the window, so she was even farther from sight. "We've got five patients who can't be moved," he told her quietly.

Carys winced. She knew that some would be stuck here, but she'd really hoped the number would be lower. "Who made the call?"

"Perkins." His voice was devoid of emotion, but which made it all the more clear he was not impressed with his assessment. Isaac might not be a doctor, but he had a heck of a lot of common sense.

"They're all on upper floors?"

He nodded.

She twisted the Claddagh ring on her pinkie. It stung.

Deep breath, Adams, same thing, different country...kind of.

"What has she been saying?" Isaac nodded toward the beautiful woman who had captured the crowd's attention.

"Right now, she has them in the palm of her hand. She's a great orator. She's saying they can't riot, because it will just end up with more innocent people dead."

"It shouldn't. Those bastards should have gone to ground with the regime change."

Carys looked sideways at Isaac and rolled her eyes.

"Okay, you're right. Nothing's ever that clear-cut here in Africa," he sighed.

"There you go."

She wanted to hit something. She should have done more due diligence before coming here. She'd taken Hamdok's people at their word that they had more say than the Transitional Military Council, that things were peaceful and democratic and that the RSF had disbanded. Instead, they had reared their ugly heads twice in the last three weeks. They attacked two enclaves outside of Khartoum; maiming, raping and killing. Sometimes, the way they chose to murder people, was to set them on fire. Carys shuddered.

The window was open so they could hear her speak even though the blinds were partially closed. They continued to listen.

"I can't make out what she's saying, she's talking too fast. Can you translate?" Isaac asked.

"She's trying to talk them into going home. She said that Hamdok will keep them safe, but some people who lived through the last massacre months ago aren't having it. They're insisting on staying here, and at the other vulnerable sites to stand guard. Besides this hospital, there's the orphanage and two schools."

"I agree with them," Isaac said.

"I don't. We're asking for a riot, which will just lead to more citizens dead."

"Bullshit," Isaac's voice was controlled. "Hamdok's people still aren't here. Hell, even the police are nowhere to be seen. They've run away like cockroaches when the light comes on. We don't know when the rebel RSF will attack next. Five days ago, they were in Sinjah, and three days before that, they were in Al Fao. They're not making any sense. They could be in Khartoum today for all we know. Have you gotten ahold of anyone on Hamdok's staff?"

She had, but she'd only gotten the runaround, they kept telling her that it was in the hands of one of the generals on the Transitional Military Council, but right now they were worried a coup had taken place.

Therefore, no one knew who oversaw the RSF—there were currently some sanctioned by Hamdok's government, and a great deal more who were not.

None of the citizens knew who they could trust. Hamdok was trying to form a coalition of forces that the masses could believe in, but it was slow in coming. Meanwhile, atrocities occurred, and the citizens took aim at anyone in an RSF uniform, afraid for their lives. Carys couldn't blame them. She didn't even know how the two RSF forces identified themselves against one another.

Then when she talked to some of her patients, they told her even the Rapid Support Forces, who had always been under the government auspices, took part in some of the rapes and killings. So Carys didn't know who could be trusted except for Hamdok himself, her security team, and the citizens. But guns, in the hands of scared neophytes, were never a good thing. They were in the deep stinky stuff.

The woman's voice rose higher as she praised the assembled citizens for their courage. She said it was because of their hearts and minds that Sudan had found peace and freedom, and it was up to them to continue down that path.

Carys waited with bated breath. She couldn't decide if she wanted the people with guns in the crowd to go home or stay and protect them from the rebel RSF members. Carys had about given up hope on any kind of military aid from Hamdok's newly formed government and watched dejectedly as the crowd dispersed.

"I'm going out there to talk to her," Carys said.

"You can't," Isaac pulled at her arm. "You're in charge, and we need your direction."

"Isaac, you can't go out there, you'll seem like you're trying to tell her what to do. Me asking questions, woman to woman, will go over better."

He finally nodded his head.

Carys hurried through the front doors of the hospital and made her way through the scattering crowd toward the truck the woman had been standing on.

"Hello?" Carys called out in Arabic.

The woman replied in English. "You're working with Doctors without Borders there in the hospital, right?" she guessed. "My name is Nasifa Alhassan. I teach at the University." She held out her hand.

Carys took it and introduced herself. "How worried should we be here at the hospital?"

Nasifa sighed. "Worried."

"Then why did you tell everyone to go home? I don't want any harm to come to our patients. I also don't want anything to happen to the men and women I recruited to come here with me," Carys said fiercely.

Nasifa gave her a steadfast look. "I don't want that either. I don't want one single person in my country to be hurt. One of my former students is with the rebels that's how I know that's the reason we're not seeing any of Hamdok's men here, they are out meeting with the RSF rebels, trying to come up with a way to make peace. Many of those men were not part of the atrocities that have occurred. Some are just young men and boys who have been forcibly recruited into their midst."

"But some of them were. Some of them are guilty of war crimes," Carys protested.

"If they can't make peace, the rebels will continue to attack our people. Peace is better than punishment," Nasifa said sadly. "At least this way, you know your patients and people will be safe."

"But any kind of peace negotiation is days away. What about today?" Carys demanded as she thought about the people in her care.

Nasifa gave her a pitying look. "You can only pray."

2

*C*ullen Lyons was the last one to enter the briefing room. He hated it when that happened. Why couldn't he have been an only child? How about the youngest child? That would have been good, right? Then he wouldn't have little sisters. Instead of taking care of them, they would have had to take care of him—that would have been great.

As he slid into a chair at the back of the room between Kane McNamara and Asher Thorne, he shuddered. Come to think of it, Chelle would have been an evil big sister. She would have tortured him to death. She probably would've tried to make him sit down at those imaginary tea parties she'd always had with her dolls and teddy bears.

"What's your problem?" Kane asked out of the side of his mouth as their lieutenant shuffled papers at the podium.

"It's Chelle. She and the guy she picked up from the

boyfriend-of-the-month-club broke up, and I was her shoulder to cry on."

"Isn't that like the fifth one this year?" Asher asked.

"Sixth," Cullen whispered. "I deleted her dating profile when she wasn't looking."

"You didn't," Kane laughed.

"McNamara, you got something to share with the class?" Max Hogan asked from the front of the room.

Cullen figured that Kane probably would have, except for the fact that one of the newer SEAL teams, Omega Sky, was peppered in with theirs. It wasn't personal, but they still hadn't earned the trust of the men of Night Storm. Maybe after they'd worked a mission together.

"Nope, nothing to see here," Kane said.

"Okay, so listen up," Max began. "Things have been heating up in Africa, specifically Chad and Sudan. Both embassies are on alert, with Chad on high alert."

"Big surprise there," Cullen whispered to Kane. Raiden Sato sat in front of them and nodded his head imperceptibly. Yep, they all knew the Boka Haram wasn't just relegated to Nigeria.

Max hit the lights and satellite photos appeared on the screen in the front of the room. "Right now, we aren't moving because we don't have any Americans in harm's way," Max explained. "But here are Boka Haram training camps in Chad. You can see they're close to the Nigerian border. According to the satellite monitoring, they've tripled in size over the last two months."

"Shit, that's bad." Kane murmured.

"Your analysis is correct, McNamara," Max said from the front of the room.

Cullen smothered a grin. Kane should have known better, their lieutenant had ears like a bat.

For the next twenty minutes, Max went over all the terrorist movements that had been captured by satellites, as well as all of the ground intel they had available. When Max hit the lights again, Cullen raised his hand and Max pointed at him.

"What's going on in Sudan? I thought things had calmed down with the election?" Cullen asked.

"The old special forces group, i.e. the Rapid Support Forces, were supposed to have been disbanded with the election of the new prime minister. They were the ones were responsible for the massacre that killed over a hundred people last summer. The war crimes trial still hasn't happened and they've gone to ground. Unfortunately, the general who oversaw all of the special forces is now part of the new government, and the people in our embassy say he's not working hard to bring his former special forces group to justice."

"So, are they still part of the current army?" Asher asked.

"Some are, some aren't. It's a rat's nest. Several cities far outside of Khartoum have been attacked. According to our sources, the new government is coordinating a peace talk with them in the next couple of days."

Cullen wrote *Fuck that noise* on his notepad.

Asher and Kane nodded at what he'd written.

"But Chad is still the one that we're most worried

about?" Ezio Stark, the second-in-command of the Omega Sky team, asked.

"That's the one the brass is telling us to focus on," Max confirmed.

Cullen heard the slight hesitation in his voice. Obviously, his spidey senses told him that Sudan was going to blow up first.

Good to know.

Max nodded his head toward the lieutenant of Omega Sky, Kostya Baranov. He'd been leaning back in his chair up front, but at Max's nod, he unwrapped his towering frame and stood up.

"My hope is that these problems in Africa come to nothing and we can keep playing in our normal Middle Eastern sandbox. Gray Tyler of Black Dawn has been telling me about all the fun he and his team have been having lately, and I would hate to miss out on anything." Kostya's smile encouraged everyone to join in with his laughter. He had a good way of easing tense situations.

When the laughter stopped, he continued.

"Then there's Mason Gault from Midnight Delta, I think I heard he and his team just got back home to Coronado, and I'm going to bet he's already been out surfing. But after that last damned mission, I think he and his men deserve to go to Fiji."

That was met by silence. Kostya winced. He knew he'd stepped in it.

Max spoke up.

"Clint Archer made it home. That's the important thing. He has good people surrounding him, and the best care in the world. I've been talking to Mason. He's been keeping me in the loop. As soon as we know everything, I'll let all of you know."

Kane and Cullen exchanged glances. They didn't have to wait for Max, because another one of their Night Storm team members kept them informed. Since Zed Zaragoza had recently been badly injured, his wife was in an exclusive sisterhood who banded together and provided support to one another. Therefore, Zed knew exactly what Clint's prognosis was on a daily basis as his wife, Marcia, stayed in touch with Clint's fiancée, Lydia.

"People, I apologize," Kostya said. "I've been spending too much time mired in meetings with the brass, and apparently, have my head up my ass." Everybody could tell he was less than happy about it. They all knew there was political bullshit going on and it was Baranov's former team had been caught in the crosshairs. No wonder he'd fucked up about Clint.

Cullen looked around and saw every one of Kostya's people sitting up straight. Clearly, they had their lieutenant's back.

"Back to Africa," Max continued. "One last thing I want to leave you with. Both embassies have teams that are extremely seasoned. If they are raising flags, then we need to pay attention. Things are changing out there, so stay close to base, you could be called in on a dime. Got that?"

Every head in the room nodded.

∾

How hot was hot? Carys pulled the scarf up over her nose and mouth, trying to keep out the sand and cover her cough. It was just a dry cough that always hit her when she was in one of these uncovered trucks going at high speeds. At least her sunglasses kept the grit out of her eyes. They'd been driving for over an hour to get to the clinic. Carys knew from what Perkins had told her the trek usually took three hours.

The closer they got to the Rufaa, the more farmland she saw. Sudan was such a dichotomy. Khartoum was a modern city, at least parts of it, all gleaming steel, but then there were the poor parts. As they drove down the highway out of the city, they passed desert, but finally she looked out in the fields and saw many people—including small children—out in the hot sun doing backbreaking work. Especially on the low-lying crops.

"What's that?" She pointed as she asked Jamal, the man driving the open-aired truck.

"What?" he yelled in Arabic.

"The crops. What are they growing?"

"Maize, sorghum, and millet are the tall stalks. Over there is cotton and peanuts," he said, pointing to the left side of the road. When she looked closely, she saw men and women amongst the stalks with scythes cutting at the taller stalks. Where they were going was very poor, so she was grateful to see that there was food to be had.

"How many people own farms?"

Jamal grimaced. "Not many, and those that do are very lucky. Much of the land around here was bought by big corporations. Soon you will see modernized harvesting techniques."

"I don't understand," Carys said. She'd heard about some land grabs, but she'd thought it had been about mineral rights and oil. "Who are the corporations? I thought the farmland passed down from generation to generation."

"Many small farmers couldn't show proof of ownership. Under the old dictator, Bashir, our government did a massive land grab, then sold hundreds of thousands of acres to the highest bidder. Pretty soon you'll see large modern farms that were sold to the Saudis. But not just them—many nations across the Middle East have bought up thousands and thousands of acres of our land to feed themselves. That is one of the things we are praying our new prime minister will fix."

The fertile farms whizzed by as the truck picked up speed. Carys was able to breathe now that they left behind the sand and dust. Instead, she was surrounded by the fresh air of the Blue Nile and the burgeoning greenery.

She sat back in the truck and wished her body temperature down as they went on for more kilometers and considered everything Jamal told her. She hadn't appreciated just how fertile parts of Sudan were when confronted by some of the malnourished patients she cared for on a daily basis. The hospital she'd been working at was for the indigent, whereas very close by were two large hospitals for the wealthy members of Khartoum society. To think that they sent so much of their food across the Red Sea to neighboring countries, while they starved, was outrageous. The inequities all around made her furious.

The truck slowed down and she looked around. They'd driven past the city of Rufaa to the small clinic. The area around the sandstone brick building was nothing but dirt and dust.

"We're here," Jamal pointed out unnecessarily. Carys got out of the truck and was surprised to find it took a moment to get her legs moving. Then she realized that she had been tensed up on the drive with Jamal's erratic driving style, so her muscles had locked just a tiny bit. She reached in to pull out her RISK kit, but Jamal wasn't having it.

"Let me, Doctor."

She gave a self-deprecating smile. She knew better than to try to carry things on her own with Jamal around, but she hated having her Rapid Intervention Surgical Kit in anybody's hands but her own.

"Thank you, Jamal." She started toward the front door.

"Wait," Jamal called as he pulled his gun from his trousers. Even after seven years of working in hotspots around the world, Carys was still taken aback at everyone's ease with guns. Not that she didn't have one herself, she thought wryly.

Jamal wasn't one of the men on her security detail, but Isaac had recommended him as a good man to be her driver.

"Dr. Adams, please go behind the truck while I go into the clinic."

She hated this, but agreed with his assessment, so she did as he requested.

It seemed like forever before he came back out with a hunched over, wizened man.

"Dr. Adams, come and meet Dr. Nazer."

Carys came out smiling with her hand extended, but inside she was concerned. This man looked to be on his last legs. She thought Perkins had told her a younger doctor oversaw this clinic.

"Thank you for coming," Dr. Nazer said in English with a British accent. "I could greatly use your help."

"Whatever you need, I'm here for you," Carys said.

Dr. Nazer started to cough, and it wasn't a dry cough, it was a deep bronchial cough. It didn't sound good.

"Should you be up?" Carys asked.

"No," he smiled. "But right now, I'm all we have until Kenneth gets back. He left yesterday to help at a farm where two men were working to get a corn hopper unstuck. When he called last night, he told me he was able to save part of one man's arm."

"Shouldn't they have come here?"

"No, he needed to do the work on-site, and he's arranging for them to be treated well enough so they can get to Khartoum without going into shock." He looked up at her from the corner of his eye and winked. "Maybe if the men are lucky, they'll get another pretty American doctor like you to work on them, huh?"

That took Carys aback, normally in a Muslim country like this, she would not expect a man to openly flirt with a Western woman like her. He must have seen her look of surprise.

"I studied at Oxford in England," he explained.

"Ahhh," Carys smiled. "I wondered."

"Please call me Rashad and come inside. Not that it will be much cooler, but at least you will be in the shade."

"When will Kenneth be returning?"

"He should be back tonight. Tomorrow morning at the latest."

Jamal followed them into the dim light of the clinic. They went down a short hallway before it widened into an open room that seemed to double as a reception area and clinic for simple procedures by the look of things.

The number of people inside surprised her, considering how empty it had been outside the clinic, but now that she thought about it, who would have wanted to be outside in the afternoon sun if they could at least be in the shade? What's more, she watched a young girl give all the people sitting against the walls and on chairs cupfuls of water from a jug. There was even some bread to be had. Fine service indeed.

As usual, there were mostly women and children, but occasionally a man sat inside, looking ready to topple over. Three women dressed in white administered to them. They had small cots set up where people either sat or were lying down and being questioned, poked, or prodded. It was a medical assembly line, with only an occasional whimper or cough coming from an ill child. What Carys would have given to hear the cacophony of complaints and noise from a US emergency room because then she would know she was dealing with a healthier group of people.

Looking around, she saw a door and another hallway.

"What is behind that door?" she asked Rashad.

"One is an office that Kenneth and I share, but we also have the nurses use it if they need to speak to a patient confidentially."

"And the hallway?"

"Follow me."

She was only halfway down the hall when the smell hit her. It was the miasma of odors emitted from healing, infected and dying flesh. Some smelled sweet, some sour, some putrid, it was a stench she was familiar with since practicing medicine in Africa. They were obviously going to the surgery ward.

There were windows along the ceiling letting in plenty of light to help the surgeons see, while operating. Bare lightbulbs that weren't currently on, hung above the area set up as the operating room. Every attempt had been made to make the space as sterile, functional, and professional as possible. As a matter of fact, compared to most set-ups she'd seen over the years, this was one of the best.

"Better than you thought, huh?" Rashad's cracked lips smiled broadly.

She grinned back at him. "Very impressive," she agreed as she moved toward one of the four occupied beds. Only one patient was conscious, and she looked at Carys curiously, despite her obvious pain.

"May I?" Carys asked the old doctor.

"Go right ahead. One of her broken ribs punctured her lung after she fell off her boyfriend's motor scooter."

Carys raised her eyebrows. A motor scooter in this part of the country was rare.

"He has many girlfriends," Dr. Nazer sighed. "His father is a manager at the large Saudi farm. The boy has more money than sense. I've delivered five of his children, from four different girls," Rashad continued in English so the girl in the bed couldn't understand.

"How is this one doing?"

"She developed an infection. As a matter of fact, everyone here has developed an infection. It is the reason I have asked for you to come here. It is my understanding that you have seen something like this in your time in Nigeria. Kenneth is a smart doctor, but he is a general practitioner, neither of us are good with infectious diseases."

Carys pulled the chart that was lying underneath the bed.

"She's not coughing," she said referring to the cough that the old doctor had.

"No, that's not the type of infection. It's bloodborne," he said just as he went into a spasm of coughing. The woman in the bed looked at him with concern. Finally, he stopped coughing and looked up at Carys, his expression filled with shame and amusement. "Our girl here is smarter than I was," he said in Arabic. "You never smoked, did you?" he asked the girl.

She smiled shyly and shook her head.

Rashad turned to Carys, "Two packs a day all the time I was at Oxford. It continued for years. Now I have COPD. I'm lucky it hasn't turned into lung cancer, but this is pretty debilitating."

Carys frowned. "You know you shouldn't be here," she admonished.

"It's where I want to be. I'm close to my sister and her children. I was foolish in my youth. Do you smoke?" he asked her. "Of course, you don't," he answered before she could. "Smart girl."

Carys shrugged. She wasn't here to pass judgment on anyone. Carys looked at the girl in the bed and saw that she was watching the two of them with wide-eyed fascination.

"Go to sleep," Rashad said kindly. "One of the nurses will be back to check on you later."

She nodded. The doctor turned back to Carys and continued in English.

"So now that we've ruled out my cough as part of the infection, let's get down to our problem with the patients. As I was saying, it's bloodborne. Kenneth has done a lot of testing."

"What has he tested for?"

"HIV, Hep B, Hep C, syphilis and malaria," the doctor held up a finger on his right hand for each item he named off.

"Those would have been my choices. Can I ask you a couple of questions?"

He nodded.

"What are your handwashing protocols?"

He called in the head nurse who talked her through how they went about washing their hands, then Carys asked about the linens and wiping down the beds themselves. Everything she heard impressed her. They'd even gone to the point of boiling all the linens and wiping down every hard surface with alcohol. These women were bound and determined not to have their patients die.

"It's been very frustrating," Rashad said. "We can't figure it out. Kenneth has been racking his brain. We've been lucky so far that nobody has died yet, but it's only because we've been able to get stronger dosages of antibiotics from Khartoum." His voice was laced with a deep level of concern.

"That was another reason why Kenneth decided to go to the men at the farm instead of having them come here. We double- and triple- checked our every sterilization method we can think of. We've even taken to boiling our own clothing, and before you ask, all of our surgical instruments go through the autoclave twice now."

Carys perked up.

"You have an autoclave? You don't boil your instruments, like everything else?"

"One of the village elders moved to Germany, but he didn't forget about us. He donated money for this clinic, and he bought the autoclave as well as two looms for the women of our village and a large oven for the community house. He has also purchased three generators for the village and regularly supplies us with propane."

"He sounds like a good man," Carys said as she smiled at the concerned nurse and doctor.

"He is."

"Can I see your autoclave?"

She saw the two of them, as well as Jamal, give her an odd look. They must have thought it was funny that the American doctor was more interested in seeing a piece of machinery than more of the patients, but she had a sneaking suspicion what was wrong.

"It's here," Rashad pointed proudly. She could see that it had been given a place of honor on a high dresser near the back wall. It was clear that Kenneth and Rashad worked hard to keep their clinic clean and healthy, but that might be working against them.

"When was the last time this was qualified?"

Rashad sighed. "Unfortunately, it has never been qualified or validated in the last three years. I'm not sure that you would even find most of the equipment at the hospital you've been working at in Khartoum qualified, but it has all been properly maintained."

He bent down and pulled a book out of the dresser drawer. "The last time this was serviced was two months ago. We do not run many cycles. This will be good for at least another year."

Carys smiled as she took the book with the handwritten notes in it. She knew about this method. She also understood how happy some of the rural clinics were with the modern technology, sure that it was a guarantee of safety for their patients.

Unfortunately, she had seen many times where it wasn't. Times where the old ways were better.

"I'm not an expert with these machines, Dr. Nazer, so I can't determine if they are properly sterilizing your surgical instruments or not. But in the meantime, my suggestion would be to boil your instruments for twenty minutes after you run them through the autoclave."

She nodded to the machine's closed door. "Are there instruments in there right now?"

He nodded.

"Has the cycle ended?" she asked.

"Yes." He opened the door and pulled out some forceps with a clean cloth that was sitting on top of the dresser, and then placed it onto a sterile surgical tray.

"I want to have this analyzed for contaminants. I think this is your culprit."

"I have something we can put this in." He found a tub of Tupperware. He asked the nurse to wipe it down with alcohol. When she was done, he placed some of the surgical instruments that would fit into the container and closed the lid.

Carys turned to Jamal. "Can you take this to Perkins in Khartoum? I'll call him on my satellite phone and tell him what tests to run."

He nodded. "Are you sure you're all right to stay without me?" he asked.

"Absolutely. Tell Perkins that I'm going to stay for a couple of days and help out. Everything is going well at the hospital and it looks like the doctors here could use another pair of hands for a few days." She glanced over at the doctor who had continued to cough on and off throughout the tour. He was going to need to be put to bed before long.

"That would be welcome," Dr. Nazer agreed.

Jamal took the plastic box and nodded. "I'll unload your things," he said.

She nodded.

"Why don't you talk to our patient with the punctured lung while I discuss our new sterilization techniques with the nurses?" Dr. Nazer said.

Carys nodded.

It was nightfall when a dilapidated car pulled up to the clinic in a wave of dust. Carys watched as an old man almost fell out of the driver's seat. He didn't look like someone who should be out of bed, let alone driving on dark dirt roads. He heaved in a deep breath and tried to yell something in Arabic, but it came out a hoarse whisper.

She ran up to him, but he shooed her away. He made it clear that he didn't want to talk to some strange white woman he didn't know. He wanted to talk to Dr. Nazer. She hustled inside to Dr. Nazer's office where he was asleep on a cot. Quickly she explained the situation and he got up to talk to the old man.

Faizah, the nurse who was going to house Carys for the night, came up to her and said she would be leaving in an hour. Carys had watched her work throughout the day and had been very impressed with her abilities.

For that matter, everyone at the clinic had been outstanding. They were caring, professional and kind.

"Let me help," Carys said as she picked up a bedpan. She might be a surgeon, but when you came to Africa to help, no task was too menial, you pitched in. Faizah and the other nurse grinned as the work went faster.

"Inaya and her husband will be here soon to take over until morning," Faizah explained. "We try to have everything done for the woman who works the shift at night."

"Dr. Adams?" Dr. Nazer called from outside. "Please come. Bring Faizah as well." They looked at one another, and Faizah shrugged as she handed the sheets she was folding to the nurse's aide.

This should be interesting, Carys thought. The old man didn't want to have anything to do with her, why was Dr. Nazer having her come back out when her presence bothered him so much?

Nazer and the older man were arguing hotly when she and Faizah walked outside. Even though it was nine at night, it was still hot. For just a moment, Carys caught a slight breeze and she lifted her face towards it, trying to block out the men's voices. She knew they were arguing about her. Wasn't the first time and wouldn't be the last time.

Faizah gave a heavy sigh. "You are a very wise doctor, yes? You have already helped to find out why the patients were getting sick during surgery," Faizah's expression was filled with admiration. "Our old ones can be set in their ways. They don't like change."

"Don't worry, the same thing happens in my country," Carys smiled. She hadn't thought about it in a long time, but she remembered her great-grandmother and some of the comments she had made when Carys had been young. Change took time.

"He needs you. It is bad. Will you go?" Faizah asked.

"I haven't been listening," Carys admitted. She had been trying to block out the argument once she realized it centered on her.

"I want you to both go," Dr. Nazer said. "Faizah, you will make the situation more comfortable for Dr. Adams. There is a woman in need, who lives at least two kilometers from him. She has three young daughters. He does not like her husband, but her eldest daughter begged him to go for help. He made this trek because the woman has been in labor for over a day. He thinks the woman will die and the girl children will try to come and live with him and his wife because the father is never around."

"Why hasn't the midwife helped?" Faizah asked. Carys wondered the same thing.

"Umar said the midwife was not available."

Carys and Faizah exchanged a glance. This did not seem right. It sounded as if this woman had been ostracized from the community.

"Of course, I'll go, but Faizah can stay here, her children need her."

"My daughter and son are old enough to stay with their father. I will go. Come, we must hurry." She headed for the car. Who was Carys to disagree?

"Let me get everything." She went inside and

looked over everything she'd brought with her in the RISK kit. She grabbed what she needed.

"Let me help," Rashad squatted down beside her in the dim light. He had a smaller sturdy case for her to use and carefully placed bags of saline from the clinic's storage. Carys grabbed the fetal heart rate monitor, and all the meds she'd need; antibiotics, anti-nausea meds, pain medication in tablet form, anti-inflammatories, as well as vials of morphine. She grabbed a handful of syringes and needles.

"I suppose you're going to want to take your own surgical instruments?" Rashad laughed at his own joke, then went into a long bout of coughing.

"Dr. Nazer, go back to bed," Faizah admonished. "Dr. Adams and I will take care of this." Carys drowned them both out as she grabbed the tubing for adults and infants, antimicrobial washes, alcohol wipes and whatever else she could think of that would fit into the case. Then she shut it.

Her backpack sat in the corner of the surgery, and all she'd grabbed out of that so far had been a bottle of water and a protein bar. She'd eaten with the staff for dinner. She looked up. "Faizah, do you have everything you need?" Carys asked.

Faizah held up a cotton tote—apparently, she traveled light.

"Okay, let's go." The nurse tried to grab the kit from her, but she wouldn't let her.

"I'm much bigger than you are, Doctor," Faizah argued.

"Fine, you can carry my backpack." The woman grabbed it and they went out to the car.

Faizah pushed back the front passenger seat so Carys could crawl into the back.

Here goes nothing.

Carys winced when she banged her knee against a piece of metal that stuck out from the back of the driver's seat.

Well, at least when she got in the back seat, she couldn't see the old man glaring at her anymore.

"Father, where are you taking us?" Faizah asked the old man deferentially.

"Far away. To the woman's shack. We must hurry."

Sitting in the backseat, Carys held on for dear life.

3

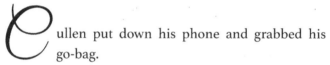

*C*ullen put down his phone and grabbed his go-bag.

He looked around his house and whistled. Aries skidded to a stop in front of him. "I don't know, Boy, that was almost five seconds, are you slowing down?" he asked.

His German Shepard gave him a grunt of disdain— there was no way he was going to take that kind of smack talk from him. After all, Aries knew who the superior being was in this house, and it sure as hell wasn't Cullen Lyons.

"Gotta go, boy. Baily's going to be coming to take you for a walk tonight."

Aries barked. The damn dog was smiling at him.

"You traitor, I knew you liked my little sister better than you do me. Do you like Chelle better than me too?"

He barked twice this time.

"You're an ass."

Aries wagged his tail.

"Next time I barbeque steak, you're not getting any," Cullen groused. He did a quick sweep of his house and saw that everything looked in order. Aries lunged toward the sliding glass door near the kitchen.

"Nope, it's not playtime until Baily's here." Hell, even when Baily was here, he wasn't always happy that she let Aries have his freedom outside with the door open, but he knew that she did. Of course, his little sister was armed and dangerous. She was the bloodthirsty one. Chelle, on the other hand, wouldn't pick up a gun if her life depended on it. Hence the reason he didn't ask her to housesit on his new lot of land out in the boonies. It had been too good of a deal to pass up, and it was exactly what he'd always wanted, but it was isolated, and he didn't feel one hundred percent comfortable with Chelle staying here alone.

He picked up his duffel and Aries came bounding over to him. "I'll be back, Buddy."

Aries came over and pawed at his bag. "Oh, now you give a damn," Cullen laughed. The dog took the bag in his teeth and pulled.

"Stop it," Cullen said without heat. When Aries kept at it, Cullen sighed and gave the command to stop and sit. Aries immediately complied.

"Good boy." He gave his head a rub. "I'm going to miss you, Buddy." He set the alarm and left the house. He really needed to unpack so he could park his Jeep in the garage, but it just seemed like something better to do, kept coming up. He shook his head and got into the Jeep and took off down the windy tree-lined road.

He was at the top of the hill when he saw Baily's piece-of-shit Buick. She waved at him as she sped by him. Thank God he had checked over her car last week, especially the brakes, otherwise he'd have to follow her back to his house to make sure she was safe.

Sisters.

Cullen was surprised to see when he got to the airbase at Norfolk that he was ahead of half the team, but then he found out the others had been at a concert. Really? Who in the hell liked country music and would actually pay to attend an outdoor concert in Virginia Beach? For God's sake, the mosquitos had to be hell.

Jazz. Now that was music.

"Not into the *Ladies*?" Max asked as Cullen set down his bag in front of him.

"Huh?"

"Lady Antebellum, that's who's playing at the amphitheater tonight. Kane took A.J. to the concert, and Leo and Asher brought dates."

Cullen looked down at his watch. They had another twenty minutes to get their asses here. "They're not going to be driving their dates home, so do you know how they're coordinating things? I can't imagine Leo letting anyone drive his truck."

Nick Hale walked up to them. "I just spoke to Kane. A.J. and the women are staying for the rest of the concert, then she's going to arrange to get Asher's car back to his place as well as the girls back home."

Cullen frowned, trying to work out the logistics in his head. He gave up. He knew that somehow A.J. had it under control. Kane's fiancée was able to manage any type of situation that life threw her way. Hell, he'd seen her manage a literal circus in the Middle East.

"So where to, Lieutenant?" Cullen asked as he saw the Omega Sky team gathering around their leader.

"Our two teams are going to be splitting up. The shit hit the fan in both places at the same time."

"Sounds about right," Raiden Sato said as he walked up. "When it rains, it pours."

"I don't think rain has anything to do with it where we're going," Cullen smirked.

Raiden nodded his head in agreement. "So, Max, are we taking off as soon as the party-animals get here?" the man asked.

"Roger that. This is going to be the last mission without an additional man. Baranov pulled together Omega Sky after his old team was disbanded. He's got a couple of men he's recommending to me. We're going to train with them when we get back and determine who would be a good fit."

Cullen looked over to the loose circle at the other end of the tarmac. He had a couple of suggestions, but he highly doubted that Kostya would let them be released.

"Hey, are you ready to get this show on the road?" Asher Thorne called from across the airfield. The man was a loud bastard when he put his mind to it. All of them turned to look. It wasn't often he saw his teammates dressed up in button-down shirts. Hell, was that gel in Kane's hair?

"Hey, pretty boy, I don't think you're allowed on the plane looking like that. You're going to be the first one the enemy shoots at."

As the men jogged towards them, Raiden Sato took a step backward. "I smell perfume."

"Fuck you, Sato." Leo sighed.

Kane and Asher laughed. "We had to sit downwind of his date, between the big hair, high heels, claw-like nails, and perfume, she stood out like a sore thumb."

"Hey, she had a couple of assets," Leo protested.

"They were fake, and she barely had them covered," Asher said with disdain. "You're not really intending to see her again."

"I'm sure not going to take her out on any more group outings, that's for damn sure," Leo said.

Kane let out a deep chuckle. "That's probably for the best, A.J.'s going to give you shit for months as it is. I don't think she was impressed."

"We can't all be so lucky as to find a woman while we're on a mission," Leo griped.

Max held up his hand. "Okay, enough fun time. We've got a job to do."

"I'll just be glad to finally see some animal besides a damn camel," Asher said as he hoisted his duffel higher on his shoulder.

"Hey, you get to see "Lyons" damn near every day," Cullen reminded him.

"You walked right into that one," Raiden shook his head at Asher.

"Please, Max, I'm begging you, fill us in on the mission," Kane said. "Don't make me listen to this shit anymore. Cullen actually thinks he's funny."

"Get on the damn plane. We've got fifteen hours to talk. Hopefully, we won't have to hear about Leo's love life or any more smart remarks from Cullen." Max jerked his chin toward the plane.

"Good God! Get your head down!" Cullen grabbed the private security man he'd met twenty minutes ago and shoved him to the ground. He didn't know why he bothered saving his life. If he was so stupid as to pop his head up for a second time, like a meerkat coming out of its hole, while they were in the middle of a gunfight, he wasn't going to live long anyway.

"Thanks, man," Hans shouted above the gunfire. "Why are they shooting? I spoke to them two hours ago, they said they were going to leave."

Cullen looked at him like he had grown two heads. Didn't he realize he was trying to negotiate with butchers?

Where was this bastard from, the moon?

Asher glared at Hans and pointed at the floor. "Pick up your gun and start shooting," he yelled.

"Oh, right."

Cullen prayed to God that things were better for Max and Nick at the embassy. At least *they* were working with Marines, and not civilians!

"How many did you say were working with you?"

Cullen asked again as he took another five shots at the targets that peeked out from behind the barricades. He needed to keep the assholes occupied while Raiden made his way to the hospital rooftop and eventually took his shot at the sniper in the building across the street. They'd been pinned down long enough. It might have been only twenty minutes, but anything over two minutes was too long as far as Cullen was concerned.

Once Raiden was in place, he could give Kane and Leo some direction since they were still at least three blocks over. How had this turned into such a shit-show so fast? He looked over at Hans and remembered why. Seriously, how had he ever been hired out as private security? He was supposed to make a situation better, not throw gasoline onto the fire.

"Answer the question," Cullen shook Hans' shoulder.

"What question?"

"I asked you how many men do you have working with you?"

"There's four of us, but Roger's already dead." Hans' words came out shaky. For that matter, so was his aim.

"Stop shooting, you're useless. Go over it again; you went out and spoke to the RSF rebels, why did you do that?"

"The police were finally here. I figured it was safe. So, I took a chance. I told them they had the wrong place, there were hardly any doctors here, I figured they would go away. The police pulled me back, and then the rebels just opened fire."

Jesus.

Hans popped up again and took another shaky shot. He almost hit the wall instead of shooting out the window into the barricade.

"Just sit your ass down below the windowsill and keep answering questions." They needed intel. By the time they'd arrived, the hospital was already surrounded.

Cullen and the rest of the Night Storm team had been informed that the peace talks between the newly formed government and the rebel RSF had broken down in a big way. One of the generals on the Transitional Military Council had been murdered. Shot in the face. Now they had yet another man calling himself the General in charge of the *real* and *good* Rapid Support Forces. But nobody really knew who could be trusted.

"So, Roger is dead, who's alive on your security team?" Cullen yelled above the gunfire.

Please God, say they were of more use than Hans.

"There's Isaac. Then there's Kip."

"Where are they?" Asher demanded before Cullen could.

"Upstairs," Hans mumbled the answer as Cullen took three more shots. "They're positioned on the south and north sides of the third floor, or it could be the east and west, I'm not sure. They said they could protect the patients and fire at the rebels. Isaac sent me down here when he saw you plow through rebels' barricades into the hospital lobby with the armored truck."

"Wait a minute, I thought you said you were in charge," Asher questioned as he looked over the windowsill and took another shot. Cullen watched with satisfaction as another rebel went down.

"I am," Hans said.

It looked like the rebel forces might be pulling back. At the very least, they were waiting on their sniper to take them out.

Fools. They were leaving their flank open and their sniper was going to bite it soon. He didn't stand a chance with Raiden Sato holding a rifle.

Hans started to get up. "It's over, right?"

Cullen shoved Hans so hard that he skidded down the wall onto his butt.

"Sit your ass *down*! I'm not going to tell you again. The next time I'm going to watch you die and figure it's for the best because you're too much work to keep alive."

It was time to contact Kane and Leo. At least the dumbass had the good sense not to say a damned word while Cullen reported into Kane.

"Yeah, Raiden's been on the roof for about two minutes," Cullen confirmed. "Apparently, we have two of the Doc Without Borders security forces helping us out on the third floor. We have one..." Cullen glanced over at Hans and decided to be nice. "We have their C.O. with us. He's along the lines of Anderson from BUD/S."

"Are you shitting me?" Kane asked through the comm. "Are his other two any better?"

"Don't know. All I know is that Asher and I have stalled the rebels for a minute, and Raiden said that he has his sights on the sniper's location. If you or Leo would be kind enough to flush him out, that would be really helpful," Cullen said sarcastically.

"Raiden!" Kane snarled into the shared comm.

"Do you see the bank building to the right of the Chicking Fried Chicken shop?" Raiden asked in his normal calm tone of voice. "There's a balcony on the fifth floor. If you could get some fire coming from the east so that he moves, I could take him out." Why did Raiden always sound so damn polite?

Asher stabbed his finger at Cullen before he said anything. Cullen sighed.

Come on, who wouldn't say something smartass about a restaurant called Chicking Fried Chicken? Asher's eyes were gleaming. He was thinking that it sounded like Frickin' Chicken too.

"We're on it, Kane said. Give us five minutes at the most. You'll have your diversion."

A spray of bullets went flying out into the streets from the hospital.

"What the hell was that? I thought we were on a lull?" Kane asked.

"Ah hell, it's the other two security guys," Cullen groaned.

Asher started rushing to the stairs, he was hunched over so that he wouldn't make himself a target. "I'm on it. I'll let them in on our plan. It'd be good to have us all singing from the same sheet of music," Asher said into his mic.

"Yah think?" Kane asked sarcastically. Kane was second-in-command of the Night Storm team, he had reason to be pissed off. As soon as the shooting calmed down, either Cullen, Asher or Hans should have been upstairs telling those other two men what the four-one-one was.

"My fault, Kane," Cullen acknowledged.

"Fine," Kane rumbled. "Don't fuck up again." He was breathing heavy; it was obvious he was moving fast.

"I'm in position," Leo said.

"Wait for me, Perez," Kane said over the link. "I want to make sure your ass is covered before you start shooting."

"What's going on?" Hans asked timidly. All he had heard was Cullen talking into his mic, he couldn't hear anything that had been said into his earpiece.

"We're going to take out the sniper. Then we're going to do a front and rear assault on the RSF rebels. It'll all be over in ten minutes or less."

"I'll tell Isaac," Hans said as he fumbled for his cell phone.

Motherfucker, he had a cell phone to get ahold of his subordinates the whole time?

"Yeah, why don't you warn Isaac to expect a Navy SEAL named Asher Thorne. How about warning both of your team members while you're at it?"

I didn't call him a Dumbshit. I'll go to heaven for keeping that to myself, won't I?

Cullen had kept his eyes trained on the street. Nobody had come close to the armored truck, they were still keeping back behind the barricades they had set up. There had been a few police who had valiantly tried to keep the RSF rebels away from the hospital, but their bodies now littered the space between the barricades and the front of the hospital.

There were fifteen hospitals around this area, but the reason they chose this one was due to the team of American, British and French doctors who had come at the request of the new prime minister. But according to what Max told them, the aides at the Embassy had explained, almost all the doctors and scientists were currently over at the University involved in a symposium.

When the RSF rebels realized they had fewer targets they were pissed off. So, they focused on the Doctors without Borders at the Hospital for the Indigent. And of course, it was their buddy Hans who had informed them of this fact.

The RSF rebels would do anything to make Hamdok look bad. What better way than to attack his hand-picked group of doctors that he had invited to help his newly formed democratic nation?

"I told Isaac to expect you. I told him to stop shooting, was that good?" Hans asked.

Cullen nodded. He was sick of talking to the man.

Hans' phone rang. *Please say they hadn't started shooting at Asher and were injured.* Asher would feel like shit if he had taken out one of the good guys.

Hans listened for a moment. Cullen continued to listen to Hans' side of the conversation. "It's bad here. We have some of those American special warfare types here. I think they are Delta Ranger SEALs or something. They didn't come in time to save Roger.

They came through the barriers with an armored truck."

Hans listened some more. It took everything Cullen had not to rip the phone away from Han's ear to find out who the fuck he was talking to.

"Jamal, you'll need to go to a different hospital. Take Dr. Adams with you. Tell her it wasn't my fault this happened."

"What do you mean she's not with you?" Hans asked.

Two more minutes, and Kane should make his move on the sniper at the bank. But it sounded like they had a missing doctor. This was *not* part of the plan. According to Max, they were now supposed to evacuate all the doctors.

"Raiden, you ready?" Kane whispered.

"Yep."

Cullen heard a blast of gunfire. It stopped.

One shot rang out.

"Got him," Raiden said.

"They're spreading out. Some coming your way." Raiden said.

Cullen heard more shots. He stood up and took aim. He got two. Hans just remained huddled where he was most useful—on the floor.

"How many?" Leo yelled.

"Probably only fifteen left," Asher answered.

"Only four came this way. I'd say they're cleaned out."

"We're going to come in slow." Dusk was settling.

Finally, Cullen heard the whomp whomp of a helicopter. He looked up. It was a police helicopter.

Really?

Finally, we're getting more back-up from the police?

If there wasn't someone working against Hamdok from inside the new government, Cullen would give up his new house.

"This is suspicious as hell," Kane said over the comm. "I just contacted Max over at the Embassy. The police only arrived after the rebels were defeated. Sounds like a bunch of horseshit doesn't it? I'd say some of the police were in on it."

"We need to get our people out of here," Raiden said quietly. "Unfortunately, I have some very stubborn doctors and nurses upstairs with me."

"Fuck that noise," Cullen said. "I'll be up there in a minute."

4

"*Y*our Mama is going to be fine, Sweets." Carys looked into the two sets of big brown eyes.

Please God, say I'm not lying.

Another ear-splitting scream pierced the walls of the tin shack, and Carys' focus switched back to the woman she was ministering to. She saw the agony on her patient's face, as the cords of her neck stood out, and she screamed again.

"Faizah!" Carys looked over at the nurse who currently had her hands full with a sick, screaming toddler. The child was probably two, but so malnourished he or she looked to be a year old.

"Daughter," the woman gasped when the pain of the contraction subsided.

Carys had one hand on the woman's forehead and the other hand on her taut belly as she gasped out a breath to talk to her eldest child. She needed to be focused on giving birth, not worried about her other children.

Carys whipped her head back to look at the two little girls who looked to be under the age of seven, but who really knew? One girl was clearly the eldest. "I need your help. You must go and get more water. You must also go to your neighbor's and get milk."

"But—" the girl protested in Arabic.

"Now," Faizah said. "Go fast."

The toddler was throwing up. At least the other two didn't look sick, but they did look like they'd been abused. So did the mother; her face was a mass of bruising. The eldest girl grabbed her younger sister's spindly arms and pulled in the makeshift door that was barely hanging by one hinge.

Carys cursed the old man who hardly stopped the car long enough for her and Faizah to disembark. Heck, she'd been lucky to pull out her bags.

The old fart! What was his problem?

As soon as the girls were out of the shack, Carys pulled up the blanket covering the woman so that she could assess her progress.

"What's your name?" she asked gently.

"Shada," she breathed out.

"Okay, Shada, my name is Carys. I'm a doctor. I'm here to help. Do you know how long you've been in labor?"

"Since yesterday morning."

Over thirty hours, and not enough progress to show for it.

Out of the corner of her eye, she could see that Faizah had started to boil water and had the medical bag open. Somehow, she was doing all this while holding a baby who was sick and in pain. *God love the woman.*

The situation was bleak. After a woman was dilated like Shada was, the risk was higher for the mother to hemorrhage. That is to say, hemorrhage even more than Shada currently had.

"Faizah, I'm going to need you helping me. Have you assisted on a caesarean before?"

"Yes," was her succinct reply.

The nurse's eyes met hers. She knew the outcome was not good. She tucked the child underneath her arm. "Tell me what to do, and I will do it."

It was time to give the mother-to-be some hope. Because there needed to be hope in this room tonight. They needed to believe that things would work out.

"Shada, I'm from the United States. I have delivered hundreds of babies in my life."

"You have?" she panted out. Her doubt was clear.

Carys gripped her outstretched hand.

"There is no place for lies between us, we must tell the truth. This is difficult. But I have seen worse and the mother and child are still alive and well."

Shada took in a deep breath as another contraction began to swell.

"I need you to pant. Like this."

Carys panted like a dog, short staccato breaths.

"Now you try, Shada. You must try to not push while I wash up so that I can examine you, okay?"

The woman nodded and loosened her hand.

Carys tore loose from her grip and went to where Faizah had extremely hot water and some of the antiseptic soap ready for her to wash with. She went back and examined Shada, who couldn't help but push during one of her contractions. Her scream caused the child in Faizah's care to increase the volume of their never-ending-scream and then they almost struggled their way out of Faizah's arms. Carys blocked out the cacophony and focused on the job at hand.

In less than a minute, she was able to confirm two things—the baby was breech, and alive.

Okay.

Okay.

Next steps.

Carys took all the necessary steps before she examined Shada more thoroughly. She needed to see if there was any way possible. Any way possible *at all,* that she could turn the baby.

Please God, let that be possible.

When she felt the baby's foot in the birth canal, she knew it was game over. Shada and her child would both die if she continued to push. Carys would have to operate in these deplorable circumstances. *Pray God the other children don't return while I'm cutting open their Mama's belly.*

~

"Why the hell isn't she answering her satellite phone?"

"There's a reason, and we'll find out soon."

Cullen didn't know whether to punch his friend or to take comfort in Raiden's calm words.

They'd just left the clinic where Carys had departed yesterday on a wild goose chase with some cranky old man. Dr. Nazer was in no condition to give a good accounting of what had occurred. He was too sick.

Thank God he and Raiden had her position locked in from her satellite phone. She was only seventeen kilometers from the clinic, but they were traveling on one of the most Godforsaken roads Cullen had ever been on. At least when he was in the Middle East they didn't call trails like these roads—they just aimed you in a direction and you crossed over the desert, not bothering to try to follow in someone's previous path. But here, they needed the road so that they didn't end up in a ditch or driving the truck up a tree. What with it being the middle of the night and only the faintest impression of tire tracks to guide them, it was a crapshoot if they were even on the right path.

"Veer left," Raiden pointed.

"What makes you think that's the right way?"

"Trust me."

Cullen pulled the steering wheel and forced the truck left. One of the things he'd learned to do in the four years he'd worked with Raiden Sato was to trust the man. He never had hunches that didn't pan out. Fuck no, that was Cullen's schtick.

"How far away now?" Cullen asked after his teeth settled back into his gums from the rough ride over the broken clay still trying to dry out from last month's rainy season. At least it was better than getting stuck in the mud.

"According to the locator, we have another ten klicks."

"Try calling her again," Cullen ordered. Luckily, Raiden didn't bat an eyelash at his harsh tone, just placed the call.

"Still no answer."

"For the love of all things Holy, does she not understand that I'm an older brother and I get worried about the women in my life?"

Did Raiden just laugh?

"How are the demon twins?"

"They're not twins, thank God. If they had the ability to switch places and talk in a secret language, I would have gone insane."

Raiden didn't immediately respond. Cullen wasn't surprised—his words came out garbled because of the bumpy road—but he was pretty sure he heard a chuckle.

"What about you? Are your—"

Cullen stomped on the brake and swerved. He came within an inch of hitting something white and enormous. It didn't flinch, except for swishing its tail.

"What is that thing? A yak? A water buffalo?" Cullen honked the horn. It still didn't move.

"It's a cow."

"Nothing with horns that stick up like that is a cow. It's an albino yak." Cullen honked his horn again. He wasn't sure, but he thought it might have rolled its eyes at him. Then two more of his brethren lumbered in front of the truck.

They didn't have time for this shit. Cullen sprang out of the truck and pushed hard into the rough white hide of the ghost buffalo.

Nothing.

It didn't move a single inch.

He shoved his shoulder into its flank, then it lifted its tail.

"Oh no, you are not—"

Raiden was going to set a record because Cullen heard him laughing again. Cullen jumped out of the way as the bleached bull almost took a dump on his boot.

"For fuck's sake. You did that on purpose."

The pasty bovine let out a loud fart.

Raiden's laugh was just as loud.

"Enough! I've had enough!"

He took out his gun and shot into the ground a couple of feet away from the cows. Off they went.

Cullen got back into the truck.

"Don't say a word," he said as he pointed at Raiden.

His friend held up his hands. "I wouldn't dream of it."

Cullen found himself going even slower on the already bumpy road. Even with the brights on, he just knew that one of those damn ghost cows was bound to leap in front of the truck, and he couldn't risk it.

"Raiden, what's your gut saying? How do you think the doctor is?"

"Just get there as fast as you can but try to do it in one piece."

Damn. Damn. Damn.

∼

"He's glorious." Carys stared down at the baby in her arms. He was a miracle. An absolute miracle. She glanced up at his mother who was also a miracle.

"You're wrong," Faizah said. "They're not the miracles, you are. They should not be alive. I have never seen anything like what you did here today."

She currently had Shada on an IV with a liter of saline and a piggyback of prophylactic antibiotics. She'd already done a morphine push, hoping it would numb the next part.

Carys had already started the process of pushing down on Shada's abdomen to make sure her uterus contracted. Shada looked at her with eyes filled with pain and accusation. Carys tried to explain why this was necessary, but the young mother didn't understand, and Carys felt like a deplorable human being.

Typically, the mother and baby would bond with skin-to-skin contact, but that wasn't possible. So Carys had her shirt unbuttoned and the little boy was only partly wrapped up in one of her clean shirts from her backpack so that he could cuddle against the bare flesh of her chest. After doing her painful duty with his mother and having her look at her like a monster, it felt good to hold the boy close.

"This little girl is not doing well," Faizah said as she tried to calm the wailing toddler. They had found out from her older sister that she was two-and-a-half years old, but she looked only a year old. When Faizah had examined her, she found fingerprints around her abdomen.

Carys needed to examine the child but she'd been too busy operating. When the older children came back, Faizah questioned who had done this to their younger sister and they had clammed up. But they had suffered abuse as well. It looked like the middle sister had a broken arm that had never been set correctly, and then there was all the facial bruising that Shada had. Carys was ready to kill the man who had so viciously abused this family.

"Let me see her." Carys and Faizah worked to trade their charges. It was easier than it would have been five hours ago. Carys just wished that the girl was struggling as much as she had been when they had first arrived. Unfortunately, she had lost strength with each passing hour.

"Oh, my love," Carys attempted to soothe little Farida, but she wasn't having any of it. She put her down on the communal bed that the children shared. She struggled weakly when Carys examined her bruised belly. Tenderly, she touched the baby girl's bruised flesh, and she could feel the heat emanating from it. Farida let out a loud howl just from the gentle touch. Carys turned her to her side so that she could see where she had been manhandled. It was obvious she had been squashed by large hands. The bruising exactly matched a large man's fingerprints.

"There is a truck coming. It's soldiers. What will we do?" The eldest girl grabbed her middle sister and shoved her into the corner of the shack and stood in front of her, her entire body trembling. Faizah did not look much better, she clutched the newborn close to her body and stared at Carys.

"What if it is their father?"

Carys looked over at her medical kit. There wasn't a chance in *hell* she was going to let that man in the house. She scooped Farida off the bed and went to her eldest sister.

"Honey, hold her," she said calmly. She needed to keep everyone calm. The girl nodded as she took her little sister in her arms.

Carys practically dove for her backpack. She dug deep to the bottom, pushing through all the supplies. When she got to the bottom, she tore at the covering that hid the secret compartment that contained her gun. She grabbed her pistol and released the safety, then she spun around.

"Get behind me," she gritted out to Faizah. The woman looked at her wide-eyed and stepped backward toward the siblings in the corner. Carys stood in front of them and steadily held the gun pointed at the door. She had a love and hate relationship with the cold steel in her hands. This was one of those times when she loved it.

"Hello?" A voice called out in Arabic.

"Dr. Adams?" An American voice yelled in English.

"Dr. Carys Adams?" her name was repeated from outside. "Dr. Adams, are you in there? We've been sent from Khartoum. Jamal told us you were at the clinic, and then Dr. Nazer directed us here. I'm Chief Petty Officer Cullen Lyons with the United States Navy, ma'am. I've been sent to get you out of here, it's not safe."

They'd sent her a SEAL? She was being rescued by a Navy SEAL?

Again?

"I have an injured mother and her children with me. We need to get them to a hospital."

"Can we come in?"

She heard a whimper behind her. She realized that all of the talk in English was scaring them, the kids didn't know what she was saying.

"Can you speak Arabic?" she called through the door.

"Both my partner and I can. Can we come in? We want to help."

"It's best if I come out. Let me come out first and greet you." Carys lowered her gun.

"Are you sure it is safe?" Faizah asked.

Carys turned to her and smiled. "I'm sure. These are good men who will help us. I have friends who are in the United States Navy. I trust them with my life." She went to the wobbly door and opened it just enough to step out.

They had their truck headlights on. As soon as she came out of the hut, one of the two men went in front of the truck so she could clearly see him. "I'm Cullen

Lyons," he said. Even from where she stood, she could feel the impact of his bright smile.

"Apparently, you know who I am. How did you find me?" Carys asked.

"We were able to track you via your satellite phone," another voice came from the back of the truck.

"Who are you?"

"I'm Chief Petty Officer Raiden Sato, ma'am. I've trained as a medic if that helps."

"It does. It does a lot. Would you mind standing next to Mr. Lyons?"

"Cullen. Dr. Adams, call me Cullen. I think we're going to be in tight quarters for more than a minute. For the record, I have some medic training too. But his training is more extensive." Carys was tense until the other man stepped next to Cullen. He didn't have a smile, he seemed a lot more serious. He was a little bit shorter than Cullen, but a little broader. It was clear that he was of Asian descent.

"Okay, gentlemen, call me Carys. You're SEALs, right?"

"Yes," Cullen answered.

Some of the tension left her shoulders. She hadn't realized just how panicked she'd been about the whole situation. Without a car and with little Farida's injuries, she hadn't been sure what to do next.

"Dr. Adams?" Faizah called from the door. "Is everything all right?"

"Yes, they're friends. They're going to help us. Give me a few more minutes and then I will have you meet them," she assured the nurse.

Even knowing that they were allies, she was cautious as she proceeded forward. It was her nature. The man named Cullen must have sensed it because his smile was kind when he gently teased her. "We're 'SEAL's', Carys, we don't bite. We don't have tusks like walruses."

She rolled her eyes and walked faster. These men were really a breed of their own, how could she have forgotten?

"Don't mind him, his mouth is always running," Raiden said as he held out his hand. Carys took it and appreciated his firm handshake.

"Don't forget me," Cullen said as he held out his hand. Carys eyed it suspiciously.

"You might be a SEAL, but your name is Lyons, so I still have to be worried about your teeth, right?"

"She's got you there," Raiden said with a straight face.

Cullen ran his hand through his hair. "Smart. I like smart." He gave her a grin out of the corner of her eye. Then he held out his hand again and she shook it. "So, Carys, how bad is it inside?"

She cleared her throat. "We have a woman who just had a cesarean section two hours ago. The newborn's vitals are okay, but not ideal. Two other children, ages five and seven, are in pretty good shape, even though they have suffered from some physical abuse. But the toddler, aged two-and-a-half, is malnourished and has significant bruising on her abdomen. I'm worried about internal bleeding."

"So, the mother, baby, and toddler need to be taken

to the hospital at Khartoum immediately, correct?" Cullen asked briskly.

Carys shook her head. "The mother and newborn can't be moved yet, but Farida, the toddler, I'm worried about her, she needs to go A.S.A.P."

"Shit." Carys' eyes followed as he ran his hand through his raven black hair again.

"We're going to need to split up," Raiden said quietly.

"How upset are they going to be to see American soldiers?" Cullen asked.

"Let's go see." Carys motioned for them to follow her into the shack.

5

*Y*ou could feel the terror in the room. In some cases that was fine as far as Cullen was concerned, sometimes he relished it because it made his job easier. But to see children looking at him with horror, it made his stomach churn.

And his smile didn't seem to be getting the job done. The little girl who sneaked a peek at him from behind her little sister actually whimpered. He turned to Raiden and glared at him. Raiden shrugged. But when he looked into his friend's eyes, he saw that he was just as devastated.

He took in the room. There were the two girls huddled in the corner, one of them holding a newborn, sheltering a smaller girl. There was a young woman who didn't look like she was even twenty, holding the injured toddler. There was a thin green blanket hanging from the ceiling shielding one corner of the shack. Cullen assumed that was where the mother was.

He didn't hear any noise emanating from that area, which didn't bode well.

As if they could read each other's minds, they each slid into an easy crouch with their backs against the far wall, anything to make themselves look less threatening.

Their rifles were strapped to their backs and their pistols were holstered, but damn, he hated flaunting guns in front of kids, even if they were probably used to them. He would have loved to have left them in the car, but the situation outside was just too damn fluid for his peace of mind, and he knew that Raiden felt the same way.

"Cullen, don't you have something we can give the kids? You and your damn sweet tooth should have something good to offer them."

"Yeah, your sesame seeds aren't going to get it done," Cullen muttered. He pushed up from the wall and beelined it out the door. In his pack was the treasure trove. How could he have forgotten it? Truthfully, Raiden and the guys knew that he rarely touched the stuff, but boy did American candy come in handy for smoothing the way. Leo was the one who brought the cigarettes, and when they really needed a favor, Max was known to bring out a cigar. Yep, bribery worked.

He was back inside before anyone had blinked. Because these weren't just street kids, but actually a family in their home, he didn't just hold out his hand and offer them the treats.

"Hi, I'm Cullen. I'm a friend of Dr. Adams," he

addressed the children in Arabic. "I would like to share some candy with you. First, I wanted to see if the doctor would like some." She was holding the baby now, but she was easily able to take the candy.

Carys smiled. "I would love some, thank you for this, Cullen."

It was obvious she approved how he was going about things. He felt a zing of pleasure at her praise.

After she unwrapped the chocolate and took a tiny bite, he asked her if he could give some to the children.

"Would you like some?" she asked, turning to the two older girls still standing in the corner. At least they weren't cowering any longer.

"Yes, please," the older girl said with a hesitant smile.

His heart melted at her shy, polite response. Once again, he crouched down. Cullen held out his hand. "Here you go."

She held her little sister's hand and they hesitantly approached him and took the highly prized treat.

"Thank you," the littler girl said. She was a beauty.

"You're welcome, Honey." He watched as the older girl opened her candy bar, broke it in half and gave part of it to her sister.

"Save the other one for later," she whispered.

Over his shoulder, he saw Raiden and Carys talking.

"Hello, I am Faizah," the nurse said as she walked over. Cullen smiled as he stood up.

"Cullen Lyons," he introduced himself. "Who's this little darling?" he asked.

"This is Farida." Carys had been right, the girl didn't look well. Her eyes were glazed over and Cullen saw the bruising around her stomach where the shirt was scrunched up from her diaper.

Cullen unwrapped a piece of candy. "Do you want a little bit of chocolate?" he asked as he showed the child the sweet. Farida's eyes showed a little glimmer of interest and she lifted her arm. Cullen broke off a little piece of the candy, put it into the tiny hand and helped to guide it to the girl's mouth. His heart damn near melted when the child grinned and held out her hand for another piece.

"You've got it," Cullen laughed. He immediately gave the kid another piece.

"Ah, shit."

"Huh?" Faizah asked.

Cullen realized he'd just cursed in English.

"Should she be eating candy?" Cullen asked in Arabic.

"Right now, I'm just glad for anything that makes her happy," Faizah said.

"Lyons. Over here," Raiden said in English. Cullen gave the girl one last smile. Then pushed a couple of bars of chocolate into Faizah's hands before joining Raiden and Carys.

"What's up?"

"It was like I said outside, Farida needs medical attention now," Carys said. "Her lungs aren't sounding good to me." She was gently cradling the newborn. Cullen noted that she had her shirt unbuttoned to the top of her bra, and the baby was cuddled close to her warm flesh.

"Are you sure we can't take everyone?" Cullen asked. "I know you said the mom and the newborn need to stay here, but we can figure out a way to make Mom comfortable." He looked up at Raiden for confirmation. His friend gave him a slight shake of his head.

"There's no way," Carys said in a soft voice so as not to disturb her tiny charge. "I was on that road two days ago. She's just had major surgery. I can't allow either her or her new baby to go. They need to stay here for at least a day, preferably two or three."

She looked over her shoulder at the blanket separating the room. She looked nervous. Even after a half-hour, he could tell that nervous was not normal for her.

"Is there something else wrong with her besides her having had the cesarean section?" Cullen asked. "Is she having complications? You mentioned some other injuries. Are you sure we should wait?"

She looked up at him with an almost grateful look. "That's just it. I can't get any of the kids to speak to me about their injuries. You saw them, right?"

"They were hard to miss." It was part of the reason he didn't just give Faizah the chocolate to pass out, he wanted to see the kid's injuries up close and personal. "An adult has been abusing them. The fingerprint bruising on the little girl was obviously made by a man's hand."

Carys' expression tightened. "Yes. That is my conclusion. I think—"

"My baby," a weak wail came from behind the curtain.

Carys went quickly behind the makeshift partition and began speaking softly in Arabic. For the first time, Cullen heard the baby give a cry. He didn't know if that was a good or a bad thing.

"Faizah? Can you come here? I need your help."

"Is my Mama okay?"

"I want my Mama."

"Girls, stay here," Faizah stepped in front of the two girls before they had a chance to go behind the curtain. Raiden just barely beat Cullen as he took little Farida from Faizah's arms. Cullen crouched down in front of the two little girls.

"Little Ladies," he grinned at them. "I was wondering if I could take your picture. I have two sisters at home who would love to see you. Have you ever had your picture taken?" He watched out of the corner of his eye as Faizah went behind the curtain to assist Carys.

"I want my Mama," the youngest girl said.

"What's your name?" Cullen asked. "I bet your name is Princess."

A shy smile appeared on her face. "I'm not a princess. My name is Aamira."

"I'm Leila," the other girl said proudly. "I'm the oldest. Can we go see our Mama now?"

"Pretty soon," Cullen assured them. "But right now, I'm going to show you some pictures, and then I want to take yours, okay? Do you want to see pictures of my sisters?"

Please say he could keep them occupied.

He'd just recently scanned some old pictures of Chelle and Baily when they were young. "Girls, why don't you come over here so we can see better?"

The whole time they had been there, Raiden had stayed close to the door, but now that his hands were full with Farida, Cullen wanted to make sure he could be on the lookout for anyone coming their way. He propped open the door just a little bit and pulled out his personal phone. He used his facial recognition to open it up, then he thumbed through the photos.

"Who's that?" Aamira asked in her piping little-girl voice as she pointed at a photo of him and his two sisters. It had been taken when they were on a tree swing together out by the lake near their grandparent's home.

"That's me with my two little sisters, when we were young. Their names are Chelle and Baily." He quickly scrolled past the picture with them all eating cake to the one where Baily had just won a ribbon in a school race. He explained about the competition.

"I'm fast too," Leila said proudly.

Carys came out from behind the curtain. "Girls, you can go in and see your mama for just a moment. Only hold her hand, okay? Her tummy hurts. Do you understand?"

The girls gave solemn nods. "Go see Faizah."

"Did you leave the baby with the mom?" Cullen asked.

"Yes, it's best if they can have as much bonding and skin-on-skin contact as possible. Unfortunately, her milk hasn't come in so he's going to need formula."

"That happens," Raiden nodded.

"When I spoke to Shada, she finally told me that it was her husband who hurt her and her girls. No big surprise there. According to her, he's a soldier who has been gone for the last week and isn't due back for a while. I tried to get her to define what length of time that would be, but she couldn't pinpoint it."

Cullen looked at Raiden. A soldier could mean anything in this part of the world, and God knew what side he was playing for. "Carys, did he leave alone, or did he go with others?"

She bit her lip and her brow furled. "I didn't think to ask. I only asked what color his uniform was, and she said it was tan."

That really didn't do them a damn bit of good—both sides were wearing tan uniforms.

"It's okay, Doctor, what other information did you find out?" Raiden asked. He rocked Farida from side to side. Cullen saw that Carys was eyeing his friend with approval. It bothered him, he wanted her to only look at him with approval.

Cullen stopped short.

Where in the hell had that come from?

"I found out that she has a concussion, is what I found out. I found out that she needs to leave the bastard!" As soon as the word left her mouth, Cullen saw that she regretted it. Apparently, the good doctor didn't feel comfortable swearing.

Damn, that was so sweet.

"Carys, where is it you think she can go if she leaves here?" Raiden asked quietly.

"We'll take her to Khartoum." Cullen glared at him.

"No," Raiden looked at Cullen with that calm way he had about him. "She can't be moved. We need to take this little girl to Khartoum and get her some help, but we can't separate this family. We need a game plan."

Carys' shoulders straightened. "And we'll come up with one. There isn't a chance in heck that this family will ever be beaten again." She walked up close to Raiden and the girl in his arms. She put her hands on Farida's head and abdomen. The little girl gave a weak cough. "We've got to move fast. How fast can you get to Khartoum?"

"Not as fast as my boy Lyons," Raiden dipped his head to Cullen. "I'm pretty sure he learned from his moonshine relatives how to drive NASCAR."

"You're driving the family. I'm staying here," Cullen stated emphatically.

Raiden's lip twitched the slightest little bit.

"But if you're the faster driver shouldn't you go?"

"He's the safer driver," Cullen said soothingly as he nodded toward Raiden.

She looked from one to the other. "Oh for Pete's sake, I have to be tired to be buying into your drivel. I know SEALs. You're both safe and fast. You both probably drive Formula One and ambulances in your spare time." Carys rolled her head side to side, then pushed it far back so the long line of her throat showed, and her strawberry blond braid fell almost to her ass.

Cullen swallowed.

"How do you know SEALs, have you worked with some in the past?" Raiden asked as he repositioned the little girl so that her head rested on his shoulder.

"You could say that. There was a problem a several years back on the island of Santa Flores." This time when she stretched her neck, she kneaded it with her hand at the same time. "Things got dicey and they had to send in a team of SEALs to help us out."

Cullen had heard about that. "Wasn't there an earthquake and a prison break?"

She sighed. "Yes, that was it. My team of doctors went in to give aid, then some of the prisoners took us hostage. We were lucky, nobody died. Well none of *us* at least." The last was said in a whisper. She firmed her lips and seemed to realize that her hand was on her neck.

"Enough about the good old days. I know you men can handle anything. So, Cullen, even if your grandpappy was a moonshiner, I don't necessarily think you're the better driver. I just want to know who's staying and who's going."

Cough.

Cough.

All three of them stopped and looked at little Farida.

"Ah, shit," Raiden said as he moved swiftly to the children's shared bed. He set the girl down as she continued to cough.

And cough.

"Let me," Carys said calmly. She removed the stethoscope that had been around her neck since they'd arrived.

Raiden stepped back as Carys listened to the girl's lungs. She rolled her over and listened to her back as she continued to cough. She went swiftly to the curtained off area and brought back a pillow. She sat the girl up and patted her back as she continued to cough. Then, as only a small amount of mucus came out, she told Farida to hold the pillow and encouraged her to cough deeper to bring up more mucus to clear her lungs. Immediately the child's breathing started to improve.

"You did good," Raiden said.

"Thanks," Carys smiled up at him.

"Hey, we don't have time for the jollygasms, folks. We need to get Raiden and crew on their merry way."

Carys gave him a sideways look while Raiden grinned at him over her head. It might be in the middle of the shit, but unfortunately, his friend had kind of figured out which way the wind was blowing. Wasn't that just the stupidest thing in the world when they were in the middle of Goddamn Africa in a critical situation?

Raiden's grin got even bigger.

"I'll go explain things to Faizah and the girls," Carys said as she left the two of them with Farida.

"So—"

"Fuck you, Sato."

"I was just going to say that we needed to get the truck packed."

"That is a lie. You were going to give me shit."

Raiden's eyes gleamed. It wasn't often that he'd seen Raiden so amused. If Cullen weren't in such a twist, he would have been laughing his ass off. Instead, he had a mission to take care of, and a woman to take care of... and impress...and woo.

Ah, fuck, who used words like woo?

"Cullen. Are you okay?" Raiden asked softly. "To hear you tell it, Kane went over the edge just as fast, but to begin with, that mission was a cakewalk."

"I have my eye on the ball. I'm fine. Trust me, nothing is going to get past me."

Raiden looked at him. Really looked at him. Then nodded. "Yeah man, you've got this."

6

"*C*arys, give him to me."

Carys felt like she was swimming through an ocean. Her eyelids wouldn't open. But as soon as she felt somebody taking the little boy out of her arms, her eyes were wide open.

"No! Don't you dare," she hissed.

"Shhhh, you'll wake up Shada," the giant kneeling at her side whispered. "You need to sleep, Carys. Let me hold the baby. Just sleep, okay?"

It was Cullen. Cullen Lyons. She remembered everything now. How long had she been fading in and out of sleep? "I've got him. I'm a doctor. Going without sleep is what I do." Why did it feel like her words were thick honey being poured from a spout with too tiny of a hole? She tried to smile at the man, but it was too much of an effort.

She yawned.

Great, now she could open her mouth wide.

Ever so slowly, without disturbing the newborn,

Cullen's huge hands cupped his head, back, and bottom, then lifted and cuddled him up next to his chest. Carys gulped when she really took a look at him. Cullen was no longer wearing all the outer garments that had included his bulletproof vest, he was now down to his T-shirt. He must have done that to make the baby more comfortable.

Now she had an image of heated honey as she darn near melted at the man's feet. She tried to sit up to hide her embarrassment.

"Where do you think you're going?" he rumbled. "Lie back down, you need to rest, Honey."

Carys thought she might burst into flames when he called her honey.

What, was he reading her mind now?

"I need to go check on Shada." She pushed up on her elbows, intent to get up.

Cullen gently nudged her back down. It felt like a caress to her overheated body, or was it her imagination that was overheated?

"Carys, I just checked on her. She's out like a light. Now I understand why you're holding this little guy, there's no way she could."

"Then I need to go check on her dressing."

"I just did. I figured it was safe for me to do it, since there wasn't a chance in hell she was going to wake up and freak out that it was some strange man. I peeked, no seepage, so we're good. I might not be the team's official medic, but if you know how SEAL teams work, then you know that we all have training."

She yawned again as she nodded.

"Carys, you need real sleep, not this catnap shit."

"Do you know how many weeks I lasted on catnaps when I was a medical school resident?"

"I'm thinking that was a few years ago, and I'm sorry to say that, like BUD/S was a ways back, so was residency. Sorry, Lady, neither of us is as young as we used to be."

She snorted. "Yeah, like you'd still be on the teams if you weren't in top form."

Even in the little bit of sunlight that was coming through the shack's roof, she could see him flush. "You're right," he admitted.

She managed a wry grin. "Knew it. But you're right, I'm not as young as I used to be," she sighed. "God knows I'm a lot older than you. You're just a babe in the woods."

You better remember that too, Carys, she admonished herself.

"I doubt that," Cullen disagreed.

"I'm thirty-three," she said, figuring that would stop all this silly flirting.

"You're a youngster." He waggled his eyebrows.

She looked at him carefully. Based on his job and his rank... "You're twenty-seven, right?"

"Wrong, I'm twenty-nine. Good try, though" he grinned. "Plus, I have two younger sisters, which ages a man. Especially *my* sisters."

She rolled her eyes.

Wait a minute, I never roll my eyes. Quit flirting!

"So, we finally agree? You're a youngster. You need your beauty sleep because you've been trying to doctor the Southern Hemisphere. I should be the one who finally gets to cuddle this little guy."

Cullen's words might be all fun and flirty, but she could see the steel in those tempting blue eyes.

"He needs skin contact. He needs to feel your body heat and your heartbeat. It's best if he could be next to his mother, but she needs her rest. But he's weak. I brought powdered formula and boiled water." She looked down at her watch. "I fed him an hour ago. Are you good to change his diaper?"

"I'm a pro," Cullen bragged.

"These are cloth."

"Carys, I noticed that. You need to sleep. I need to be closer to the door. Hold him for a minute." She took him back and watched as Cullen tugged off his T-shirt. He went over to the water pot on the stove. He poured out a cupful and magically had some of her antiseptic soap and used both to wash. He pulled something out of his duffel, and she saw that it was a shirt. "It's clean," he assured her as he used it to dry himself. "Now, you know you can give me the little guy."

She was so tired. Once again, Cullen came over and took the newborn from arms that felt like lead. "Thank you," she slurred.

"Go to sleep, Doc. I've got your back."

SEALs. Gotta love 'em.

Then everything fell away.

~

Her head was exploding with pain. He was trying to rip out every strand of hair as he forced her mouth closer to his body.

It wasn't real, was it? She was dreaming? She was in Africa, not in Santa Flores. Carys slipped deeper into her dream.

God, the smell of him was making her gag. She fought the need to throw up.

Smack!

Pain burst across her cheek from where the man's meaty hand had backhanded her face. Her head was stopped from snapping back because of the hold he had on her hair.

"Whore!" he screamed in Spanish. "You better not bite me. We will kill everyone in this hospital if you don't please me."

She heard the other escaped convicts laughing and jeering behind her. The broken concrete under her knees dug into her flesh, eating into her kneecaps.

Think! You're a doctor. This is just one more emergency to solve. Think, Carys, think!

The leader smeared his semi-erect penis against her burning cheek.

More tears. Why was she crying? She didn't want him to know that she was scared and hurting. He shoved her closer to his groin and she saw her red-gold hair tangled with his wiry pubic hair. It was a nightmare. He yanked again.

She was tipping over, she grabbed at his thighs, otherwise, her face would smash into his crotch. Her fingers on her left hand trembled as they dug into the hairy flesh of his thigh, but the Claddagh ring on her right hand scraped against metal where his pants were still partially pulled up.

It was the pommel of a knife sheathed to his thigh. She didn't think, she just moved. In less than a second, she wrapped her arm tight around his leg then shoved the tip of his knife up into his scrotum. She was pleased and horrified to see his blood drizzle down his inner thigh.

"Kill her!" the leader screamed at his now silent team. She felt spittle rain down on her.

She heard one of the men behind her say that the bullet could end up killing him.

"Come closer and I'll cut off his cock," she croaked out in raspy Spanish.

"I told you to kill her," the man in her embrace shrieked. "You're two feet away. You can't shoot straight? Kill the bitch."

Carys flinched. She was going to die. But maybe stalling for time would allow the other hospital workers to get away.

He yanked even harder on her hair. She felt strands pulled out of her scalp. She clamped her lips shut to stifle her cry of pain.

"Somebody kill her! We've got to get upstairs and get with the others."

She didn't want to harm someone. It went against every oath she'd ever taken. But he was evil, and these men were just going to hurt and kill more people. She pressed the knife farther into his soft flesh.

He yowled.

"If you won't shoot, come and get her! She's killing me!" His panic was obvious.

"You keep talking and threatening me, you'll never father a child. Tell them to back off." Carys' growled the words, surprised to realize she meant every one of them.

"Just walk up and put a gun to her head, you dumbasses," the leader let out a whiny yell.

This was it, she was going to die. Would she be able to kill him? Maybe. Maybe not.

"I wouldn't do that if I were you," a man said in American-accented Spanish. "Drop your weapons or I'll kill you all."

"Don't do it, there are three of you and just one of him!" the leader screamed.

Who was he? Carys was going to throw up. Not because of the fear, but because of the stench. Breathe through your mouth.

"Don't forget her. She seems to be on my side, and she has your leader by the balls."

She let out a bark of raspy laughter.

Who was he? Where had he come from?

"Shoot him," the leader screamed so hard that he moved, and the knife dug deeper. He yowled in pain.

"I'm supposed to take you in, and return you to the warden," the American soldier said in Spanish. "If those weren't my orders, you'd be dead. Now drop your weapons."

"Shoot him."

A shot rang out from upstairs.

Oh no, they were killing her friends. He pulled her hair again. More shots behind her. She couldn't see as he pulled her hair and yanked her closer. She was going to die. Well, so was he. She plunged the knife and yanked. Hot blood sprayed across her face, hair, and hands. Carys screamed. She would never, ever be able to stop screaming.

~

She struggled as she felt a hand over her mouth. She scrabbled away from the strong grip, digging her nails into the thick wrist above the hand that covered her mouth.

"Carys," wake up. It was a commanding voice. She recognized it...barely. She was still lost in her dreams and having trouble separating the dreamworld from reality. She blinked fast, and finally, Cullen came into view. He was holding a baby.

The baby was crying, and she could hear another voice crying out weakly.

Shada.

Africa.

Navy SEALs.

Again.

"Carys, are you with me now?" His voice was now full of empathy and caring. She couldn't stand that. If he was too nice to her, she'd shatter.

She pulled at his wrist and nodded. Cullen let go.

"I need to go to Shada, are you good with him?"

He nodded again, obviously not wanting to do or say anything that might upset her fragile composure.

She pulled herself up off the lumpy makeshift bed and went in to see how Shada was doing. When she went behind the curtain, she found the woman half on, half off the bed. "Where are my children?" Carys gave a wan grin. God please the woman, she was trying to be demanding and Carys was so proud of her show of strength even though she had to be weak as a kitten. But she needed to get her back into the bed so she didn't rip her stitches.

"They're getting help. Your daughter Farida needed medical care in Khartoum, she and your other daughters went with Faizah to get some. Your new baby is here. You still need a day or two to rest before we can take you into Khartoum to be with the rest of your family."

"No! My husband is there, he will find me and kill me." She grabbed at the sweat-stained sheet. Carys made a note to switch out the sheet with the other one she had drying on the line. "Give me my baby. You must get my other children. We will go to Egypt. My mother's uncle lives in Cairo."

"Does he know you?" Carys asked calmly as she helped Shada back into the bed.

"No, but he will do the right thing." It broke Carys' heart to see the look of frantic hope on Shada's face. The woman knew as well as Carys did how many refugees ended up stranded in refugee camps when they sought asylum in other countries. Carys had worked in too many of them—even this life here, that Shada had, was better.

"Right now, you need to focus on getting well," she said to the weak woman. "Let me bring in your son."

"My baby is a boy?" she asked in awe.

"He's a healthy, beautiful boy," Carys confirmed. She stroked her fingers down Shada's wrist, subtly checking the IV insertion point, then she placed her fingers on her wrist and looked at her watch so that she could take her pulse.

"When can I hold my son?"

"In just a moment," Carys assured her. She loved

the look of love and wonder on Shada's face. She tugged the stethoscope from around her neck and listened to her heart and lungs.

"Now can you get my baby?" Shada pleaded.

Carys took off the blood pressure monitoring cuff. She was disturbed by how low her BP was. It was not good at all, and it wasn't because of the painkillers. "Shada, I'm going to need to press on your abdomen again, okay?"

Shada looked at her with trepidation. Finally, she nodded. Carys pushed firmly, doing what she needed to do to help the woman's uterus contract. Shada was crying by the time she was finished.

"All done. Now I can bring him in for a visit."

"Thank you, Doctor."

"Wait!" Shada held out her hand. She reluctantly pulled down the sheet. Then she also unbuttoned the nightshirt that Faizah had dressed her in. "I don't think my milk has come in." Her expression was anguished.

"Ah, Honey. It's all right. Sometimes it takes a while. I've already been feeding him formula, he's doing fine. Trust me, everything will be fine. Let me go get your son."

Carys went around the blanket and almost ran right into Cullen. After her nightmare, it was disconcerting to have to look upwards into the face of such a large man. Normally she would be a little bit fearful. But really, how could she be when confronted with a man who was humming a lullaby to a tiny baby?

"I heard," he whispered. "Here you go," he deftly placed the little boy into Carys' arms. "Is she good to feed him? A bottle I mean. I warmed up some boiled water, mixed in the formula and then let it cool."

Carys shook her head and smiled. She was impressed. "You did? Yes, she's fine."

He went and plucked the bottle off the rickety table. "Here you go."

"Thanks," she grabbed the glass bottle from him and ducked behind the blanket to where Shada was in bed waiting for her son. When she handed the newborn to his mother and saw the two of them together, tears welled up. She was stunned. That wasn't like her. Normally she kept it together far better than this. If she didn't, she wouldn't be able to cope with some of the things she had been forced to see over the seven years she'd been with Doctors Without Borders, but that dream had really messed with her head.

"Thank you, Doctor. You saved us."

"You did all the work," Carys said as she watched the beautiful sight of Shada feeding her child.

"I have decided on a name. I shall call him Adam."

Carys sucked in another shaky breath.

Again, with the tears?

"I am honored."

Shada continued to stroke her baby's hands as she nestled him next to her. He'd scored a nine on his Apgar test and had all indications of being a big and sturdy little boy if he got enough food. Now she watched as Shada started to whisper things into her son's ear. Carys could hear the promises she was making. She wanted a better life for her son, one without pain.

She couldn't handle it for another second, she fled out into the main area and once again ran straight into Cullen.

"Whoa there." His voice was low as his hands took hold of her upper arms and her nose was practically buried in the hard-muscled planes of his chest. Startled, she looked up and up until she was finally looking into the bluest eyes she had ever seen before. They were filled with compassion. "Carys, are you okay?"

She shook her head. Her hair had long since escaped her French braid and tendrils flew across her face. She flinched. As if he knew that bothered her, he brushed them away from her eyes and lips.

"Let's get some fresh air, would you like that?"

She nodded. She couldn't seem to get any words out.

His look was so warm, so compassionate, she felt like she could melt into his arms. It felt so odd. She had never felt like this before. Not even with her husband had she felt like she could actually lean on someone. Well, except for that time, that man, in Santa Flores. But this was stronger even than that.

"Carys, come with me," he coaxed. His hand clasped hers, their fingers entwined. He drew her outside, to a velvet night with sprinkles of stars glowing down on them. Cullen put his arm around her, and she rested her head against his shoulder.

"This isn't me, you know," she warned him.

"I know. But I think you need a little bit of care after your nightmare. Do you want to share?"

For the longest time, they just leaned against the tiny little house in the center of the world, staring up at the moon. Did she want to share with this man who she really didn't know?

"It was a bad situation. I was almost raped. Almost killed. A SEAL saved me."

Cullen brushed back another stray lock that the almost non-existent breeze had blown against her cheek. The feel of his fingers warmed a spot in her heart that had remained dormant for years.

"That sure is a short story." His smile was sad.

"It's true." Her breath ruffled his chest hair.

He pressed her a little closer to his body and she felt safer. "I didn't doubt that. Did you tell me enough to help with your nightmares, or are you going to have another one the next time you close your eyes?"

"It was a long time ago, Cullen, and with the things I see, the atrocities? I'm hard, Cullen. I've had to be rock hard to do this job. You know?"

"I know." His voice rumbled under her ear. "But after the fight, there are times the ugliness comes up and bites me in the ass. Is that what happened to you today?"

She nodded. The feel of him against her cheek felt good. She moved just a millimeter closer. That was all she would allow herself. And, as if Cullen knew, he didn't pull her any nearer, but his warmth sank into her bones just the same.

"Carys?" he prompted.

"It's been a culmination of things. I resigned. I always knew this kind of work had a shelf-life. I was in the middle of getting my life together in Oregon when Hamdok's people contacted me. I had resigned from Doctors Without Borders."

She felt his stare, felt his questions, but he didn't ask. He just waited for her to continue. Pain lashed through her as she remembered the last project she'd been on before she went home to the States to try to see if she would continue.

"What are you thinking about?" he asked softly.

"It was the Moira camp in Greece that was the last straw," she said woodenly. She wondered why Cullen sucked in his breath, then saw that her nails gouged into his chest.

"I'm sorry!" She tried to untangle herself from his embrace but he somehow managed to hold her close in such a gentle manner that it felt too good to give up, so she relaxed back against him. "I didn't mean to hurt you," she apologized.

"Yep, it was going to be the scratches from your nails that were finally going to get me that Purple Heart, and I stopped you. Dammit, what was I thinking?"

For just a second she felt like smiling. How did he manage to do that?

"Finish your story, Carys. Tell me about Greece." His voice lured the words from her broken heart.

"I revived a boy who was ten years old. It took me twenty minutes. When he woke up and looked around, he started crying and screaming. When I asked the translators what he was saying I found out that he'd tried to kill himself."

She sucked in the hot African night air, trying to brace herself. "I lost it, Cullen. What was I doing this for if things had gotten so bad that in refugee camps the children were trying to kill themselves? What good was I?"

"Jesus. I don't know what I would have done except hold him and cried right along with him," Cullen admitted.

"I wanted to do just that, but I was in the middle of a never-ending assembly line. There'd been a camp psychologist, a good woman from France, but she was in over her head, I think we all were. Just too many refugees, not enough space or resources, and no solutions. When I found him again, they were taking his father away to be buried. He had no hope, and neither did I at that point. I gave his mom everything I owned before I left to go Stateside. Marie-Clair, the psychologist, told me that the boy and his mother finally made it out of the camp. She's given me a couple of updates. But there were so many others. I just lost it, Cullen."

"So how did you get here?"

"One of my med-school friends was a surgeon in Khartoum. She had recommended me to the new prime minister to help put together a coalition with the Sudanese and international communities. After being under a dictatorship for so long, they needed a jumpstart. Prime Minister Hamdok is a very convincing man and he desperately wants a better life for his people. I figured this would be more of a coordination role and I could cope."

"But then everything piled up and you ended up here with nightmares, right?"

She nodded, her cheek sliding against the muscles of Cullen's chest. He trailed his hand down the thin shirt covering her back.

"I'm surprised the Santa Flores incident came up. That was almost four years ago, I should be past that."

Her head jerked up in surprise when he snorted.

"What?"

"If one of my sisters told me that she was almost raped and killed, but she'd put it behind her, I'd have her committed."

How can a tone be both rough and caring?

He tilted her chin up and she saw his crooked smile. "Come on Carys, you're a smart woman, you know better than that," he gently admonished.

"It's been over a year since I had that nightmare. I thought I was finally over it. I honestly did."

"And how did you manage that? Therapy?"

She couldn't keep his gaze.

"Was there someone else you talked to? A parent? A sibling?"

She shook her head, looking at the red clay beneath her shoes.

"A lover?"

She let out a long sigh, "No one."

7

*C*ullen felt like he was holding a porcelain statue. A beautiful piece of art that had been through the fire many times and ended up exquisite, something meant to last through the ages, yet could still shatter if not treated with the love and care it deserved.

He closed his eyes and prayed for guidance on how to protect this woman.

How had he always known that it would hit him like this? His dad had told him that it had taken only one day with his mother, and he was a goner. Cullen was nothing if not his father's son.

But really, in the middle of Africa?

He was expecting the grocery store. Home Depot. Maybe the Cheesecake Factory. But Africa?

She stiffened and drew away from him. Okay, now it started. He smothered his sigh.

"I must be a heck of a lot more tired than I realized. I never spill my troubles out on the first person who comes along." She pushed her hair back from her face with a trembling hand and started to tighten up her braid. "I need to get back to Shada."

She disappeared into the shack and left him looking out into the green tree line. Cullen looked down at his watch and pulled out his iPhone. Nope, no cell service, so he grabbed the satellite phone and called Raiden. No answer. Max was next.

"About damn time you checked in. I've been trying to get your ass on the line for hours," Max said. "Get the doctor to Khartoum, we're out of here yesterday."

"Max can't do it. There is no way she's going to leave her patient," Cullen explained calmly.

"You don't have a choice, because you can be sure as shit there are eyes on the both of you. Get the fuck out of there. I don't care how you do it. *Get. Her. Here.*"

Cullen toed open the rickety door with his boot. Above the static of the phone he could hear the baby crying.

"Max. The mother could die."

"Cullen, you're not hearing me. Dr. Adams has a target on her back. Four of her associates have been killed. Another two are missing. The rebel forces are making a point. They don't want this democracy to succeed and they have decided to make examples of all the aid workers. The C.I.A. found a list with Dr. Adam's name on it. You've got to get her out of there."

Cullen's blood ran cold.

"Got it."

"Do you?" Max asked. "Because her life is on the line. I understand that she feels the need to take care of her patient, but nobody should die the way Nurse Kowalski did."

"I said I understood," Cullen ground out. He didn't need to hear any horror stories. "I'm going to get her to safety. I need to get a vehicle."

"Keep me updated."

"Yes, sir," he said, then disconnected.

He took a moment to get his head on straight. The last thing he wanted to do was scare the hell out of Carys, it wouldn't do a damn bit of good. Cullen pushed open the door with his shoulder and looked over the little home. To think of it as a shack did it a disservice, not when the little girl's bed was covered with vibrant fabric and the walls had been painstakingly painted in blue and white. Hell, there was even a water glass on the little table with a wilted flower in it. Yep, this was a home, and there was a woman of the house who needed to be taken care of, and there wasn't a chance in hell that Max would have considered leaving her behind if he were in Cullen's shoes. Not a chance in fucking hell. He knew his friend too well.

"Cullen?" He looked over at Carys as she came out from behind the blanket. "Is everything okay?" she asked in English.

"I'm going to go find some transport. We need to move out."

"We can't. Shada needs at least, at the very least, another twenty-four hours of rest. Her blood pressure isn't good. She's bonding with the baby now, but even that is going to tire her out."

He moved closer and looked down at her so that he

could talk quietly. "Carys, things have changed. It isn't safe here. I'm going to go find some kind of vehicle, and when I get back here you need to be ready to go. This is life and death."

Her green eyes searched his face.

"There's really is no other choice, is there?" she asked. She must have read the answer in his expression, because her chin lifted, and her mouth firmed.

"If there were, I would take it. I promise. I've got to go right now." He started pulling on the gear he'd taken off to care for the newborn. Carys watched him with steady eyes.

"What can I do to help?" she asked.

"Have everyone ready to leave when I come back."

She nodded once. She seemed steady as a rock.

"Anything else?"

"Keep your gun with you at all times. If anybody but me, or one of my men, comes through that door, shoot to kill."

Having him gone was a blessing and a curse. She looked down at the gun in front of her on the rickety table. She had the door of the shack propped open just a little bit so she could hear if any vehicle was coming.

A headache of epic proportions was coming on so she had taken some ibuprofen—hopefully, that would do the trick. *Hopefully.*

"Admit it, you're confused and scared."

Talking things through out loud was a trick she'd

learned from a psychologist she'd worked with years ago. He'd told her that if she said things out loud, and owned those feelings, they wouldn't have as much power over her.

"I'm confused. I'm scared."

This didn't seem to be getting the job done. She jumped up from the table and strode across the room to look in on her charges. They were both asleep. She plopped back into the chair. She tried again.

"I'm confused. I'm scared."

She heard Derek's voice in her head laughing at her. He would know she wasn't claiming all her emotions.

"Cullen has me more scrambled than an omelet. Are you happy, Derek?" she hissed.

She hadn't felt this mixed-up in years. What the heck was wrong with her? Maybe her hormones were acting up.

She traced the grain of turquoise painted wood with her thumbnail and laughed at herself. Yeah, her hormones, the ones that hadn't even clamored when she'd been married for two years. Those non-existent hormones. Derek sure wouldn't believe that she was fiercely attracted to a man in less than twenty-four hours, when she'd made him wait until their wedding night to sleep with her.

Her head shot up as she snorted with laughter. She waited to see if she'd disturbed either Shada or the baby. When she didn't hear anything from behind the blanket, she went back to her thoughts. If you could call them thoughts. More like letting the squirrel loose in her brain.

What the heck was wrong with her?

Ouch!

She pulled the sliver of painted wood out from under her nail and sucked on her thumb.

She'd come a long way since those residency days when she'd tried to juggle a new marriage and starting her career. Why had she let her parents and Derek push her into that? To this very day, her parents still harped on the fact that Derek now ran his father's car dealership in Omaha and lived in the gated community with his wife and two children, and that could have been her.

They'd had the gall to have him and his wife at one of their Christmas parties when she was there five years ago—since then she'd avoided going home for the holidays. It was painful, even to take phone calls from her parents since they made it clear that she had chosen the wrong path in their eyes. Instead, when she was Stateside, she spent a lot of time with her friends David and Sarah Sloane, and a very few others.

She pushed away from the table and scooped up the gun. She hated the darn thing, but it was necessary. She needed fresh air. Thinking about her parents always did that to her. She looked up into the night sky.

How gorgeous.

For just a moment, she caught a breeze and it felt sultry against her skin, magically it seemed to heat her from the inside. Cullen, with his blue eyes and broad shoulders, heated her from the inside out, too. She shivered, not from cold, but from a long-dormant feeling of desire.

Whoa there, girlfriend. Desire? I must be tired.

She closed her eyes and leaned against the side of the house, knowing she'd hear anyone coming down the distant road.

What was going on?

"It's a phase. You're going through a phase," she assured herself.

Thinking about all the changes she'd made in the last year, quitting Doctors Without Borders, and the time she'd taken to really look at her history and think about her future, she wondered how she got to this moment. Right before she'd taken this assignment, she'd decided it was time to start an *actual* life. She'd been shortlisted for a job at a small hospital in Eugene, Oregon. She'd been in escrow for a house, it was only a few hours' drive from Sarah and David's place.

They were part of her real family. Over the years, she had realized that she could create her own family, and slowly, it had increased. A few people had slipped in fast, like two members of the SEAL team who had rescued her and a couple of doctors and nurses that she'd served with, but her actual family? Nope.

She looked down at the pistol, unable to believe she was once again in a life and death situation. What had she been thinking, coming to Africa? She knew that there was always a risk. Then she considered Shada and her swollen face. And her poor abused children, and that beautiful newborn. That's why she was here.

And maybe, just maybe, Cullen?

Those blue eyes. Was he her *actual* life?

That wasn't really possible, was it?

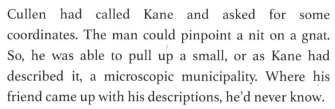

Cullen had called Kane and asked for some coordinates. The man could pinpoint a nit on a gnat. So, he was able to pull up a small, or as Kane had described it, a microscopic municipality. Where his friend came up with his descriptions, he'd never know.

"Cut the shit Kane, does it have a car, a truck, a bus? Anything? I need to transport a woman in a prone position. A moped isn't going to cut it."

"I heard you the first time," Kane said. "I'm telling you that five klicks north from where I've got you pinpointed, there's a village with a couple of trucks. You're golden, as long as you can get in there and steal them without getting killed."

"If your intel is good, my skills can keep up," Cullen assured him.

That had been an hour and a half ago. It was still an hour before sunrise, and he was staring at the two trucks in question. They were fugly, there was no other term for them. Normally when it came to German engineering, Cullen was a fan. But this looked like a VW mated with one of those albino yaks. Yep, the two trucks were Unimogs. But they were beasts. They were fantastic in all types of terrain. He bet it would do great in the Baja 1000 Desert Race, except that no American in his right mind would drive anything so butt-ugly. So yeah, he'd scored. Sort of...

He continued walking the perimeter of the small village, there were fourteen houses in all. They were surrounded by rows and rows of sorghum and millet plants, which explained why they had trucks. Score one was the trucks, score two was the plant cover and score three was making it before dawn. He saw a line of clothes hanging from a clothesline. Never passing up a possible advantage, he grabbed a headscarf, a hijab, a raggedy pair of pants that wouldn't cover his ankles but might fit around his waist and a huge football jersey for the reigning soccer team of Sudan.

They'll probably be more pissed about him stealing the team jersey than the truck.

Just before he was ready to head back to the trucks, he saw a flash of white on the ground. He grinned when he picked up the extra-large thobe.

Thank you, Allah!

With this, he could at least cover up his uniform and blend in at a distance. Now for getting one of the trucks out of here without anybody noticing.

He checked them both out, the blue truck had better tires, so that was the likely winner, but the true test was going to be which one had the fullest fuel tank.

Both were unlocked, so he went up to the red one.

"Come on, Baby, give Cullen what he needs." Quietly he opened the door of the first and carefully tipped the visor. Down fell the keys into his hand. He plugged the starter key into the ignition and turned one click. A half tank of fuel and shitty tires. *Please, please, please say the one with good tires has more petrol.*

He crept over to the puke yellow truck and opened the door. He held out his hand, tipped the visor and nothing.

"Fuck me running!" he whispered under his breath. He looked around the cab, checked the glove box.

Nothing.

"Think, Lyons."

He went to the front of the truck and swept along the front tire underneath the fender.

Thank you, little baby Jesus.

He put the key into the ignition, turned a click and saw gold. Almost a full tank of fuel and damn near new tires. He scoped out the back of both truck beds, not surprised to find full jerry cans of petrol. He grabbed the one from the loser truck and tucked it in next to the one he intended to commandeer.

Here near the side of the husking shed, the trucks were stored on a plot that was on a bit of a rise, probably to let the rainwater drain away and prevent flooding into the shed. Another bit of luck that he'd take any day of the week. He wasn't going to start the truck here, with that damned diesel engine it would wake everybody in all fourteen homes. Instead, he released the brake and put it in neutral, then started pushing it toward the road.

After the first three steps, Cullen's legs were beginning to hurt.

You should have been training more, not working on your house, you dumb bastard.

Cullen's muscles were on fire by the time he got the truck pushed to the road. As soon as it hit the thick red clay of the road, he fired up the engine and started driving, praying that the villagers would just assume it was a truck driving by. He didn't need a truck chase in the middle of Africa.

Even after a mile down the road and he realized he'd gotten away with the truck, he still wasn't happy. Not even the splendor of an African sunrise could get a smile from him, he was too worried about Shada. With every deep rut in the road he winced, worrying that she would end up ripping open her incision and bleeding out.

He slowed down as he approached the lonely house. Once again, he wondered why she lived so far away from any other person. That wasn't the norm from what he had learned at the briefings he had been given and what he had observed. Normally a family like hers would be surrounded by more people. What was the deal?

Cullen got out of the truck, prepared to see what progress Carys had made inside the house to get Shada and the baby ready for travel. Before he had even stepped two feet toward the abode, the door opened, and her hair was glinting in the sunlight.

She opened the back door of the truck. "Thank God it has a backseat. I was worried that you were going to bring me a sedan or a two-seater truck with just a flatbed in the back. This will work."

"What do you have in mind?"

"Come inside. I need you to cut some things down to size. Once you do that, the mattress will lay out pretty well. I want to give her as much cushioning as possible, but we can't use the blood-soaked bedding from where she gave birth."

It took a moment for Cullen's eyes to acclimate from the bright sun to the dim interior of Shada's home. He could see what Carys was indicating. She had piled two crates near the door, they could be cut down so that they could be shoved into the footwells of the back passenger seats and then a mattress could lay on top of the seat and the crates. He grinned. The innovation was perfect.

"Let's get this going," he enthused. "How are Mama and Baby?"

"I just administered a low dose of pain meds to Shada when I heard the truck pull up and confirmed it was you. Adam doesn't need to be fed again for another two hours."

Cullen paused from where he was modifying the crate to fit into the back of the truck. "Adam, huh?"

Even in the dim light, he could see Carys blush. She nodded.

"I think that's a perfect name," he said quietly. "So, will they be ready to move when we have this set up?"

"We will do what we have to do." She walked over to him and crouched down. "Cullen, this is one of the worst possible things we could be doing. You know that, right?"

His gut clenched. "Carys, I wouldn't be doing it if there was any other choice." He cupped her cheek. "We have to get to Khartoum—your lives, all three of your lives, are depending on this."

She nodded. "Okay, I have scoured the house. Every bit of fluid and food I've got packed. I also have a hijab for me to wear."

"You plucked the suggestion right out of my head," Cullen said as he bent back down to the crate. "Is she on solid foods? I have some MREs. Raiden stuffed his into my pack. There's packets of fruit and applesauce in there for her."

"The applesauce would be a Godsend. Maybe I could finally get her to eat something. But so far, she just hasn't been interested. That's just one more reason I'm so worried. I have a few bananas as well that I was going to mash up. We're not going to be able to take the direct route to the capital, are we?" Carys asked.

Smart. The lady was smart.

"Nope. Not with me driving. Even with you in the hijab, I'm going to stick out like a sore thumb. I'd normally suggest we drive at night so we could avoid detection, but I need to be able to see the road so that I give Shada the smoothest ride possible."

He stood up and Carys followed him as he went out to the truck to see if the crates fit in the footwell. They did.

"Is she going to be okay with me carrying her?" Cullen asked.

"That's part of the reason I administered the pain medication. Having a strange man, especially an American, carrying her was going to be difficult for her no matter how desperate the situation. I have her covered in her hijab. I've told her about you and explained that you are a trained medic like Raiden. That seemed to help."

Cullen nodded. He picked up the mattress and Carys' large medical bag and hauled them out to the truck. When he had it all situated, he went in to carry Shada out to the vehicle.

He formally introduced himself in Arabic. "Your son is very handsome."

She hugged her son close to her chest, then relinquished him to Carys' waiting arms.

"Thank you, he is already a great joy in my life," Shada said sweetly.

"It has been a pleasure to feed him and meet all of your children." Even dosed with pain medication, Cullen could see a look of pride in Shada's expression.

"Please tell me if I'm hurting you when I lift you up," Cullen asked. "The last thing I want to do is cause you any pain."

"I will be fine. Just take care of the doctor and my baby," the woman said softly.

Cullen couldn't help but admire the woman's stoic attitude. He carefully picked her up, not surprised when she didn't make a sound. Carys held the door open while holding the baby in her other arm. She walked ahead and was able to help him place Shada in a comfortable position, all without causing baby Adam to wake up.

He helped Carys into the front seat, then went back into the house to make sure nothing was left behind. As soon as he was satisfied that they were all packed up, he hot-footed it out to the truck, and headed out on the route that Kane had provided.

8

*T*he cloth that she had tucked up around the windows in the backseat helped to keep the sun off Shada and Adam as they drove at a snail's pace down some non-existent road. Carys knelt over the front seat and wrung out the damp cloth, and wiped it down the woman's brow, face, neck and arms.

"No," she protested groggily.

"He can't see," Carys reassured her, referring to Cullen.

Adam was pressed in beside Shada and the bench seat and giving a weak cry. He needed to be fed. She checked the saline drip into Shada's arm, it was still flowing.

They'd been on the road for four hours, and Carys needed to check Shada's dressing. What's more, the last time she tried to feed Adam, he just spit up the formula. The constant motion was making him carsick. Why couldn't he be one of those babies who were comforted by being driven around?

"Carys, sit forward and put on your seatbelt," Cullen said sharply.

The truck lurched and Adam sank down lower between his mother and the back of the seat. Carys had to almost stand up on the seat to pull him up.

"Carys, goddammit, sit your ass down."

She ignored him, then picked up the now squalling child and maneuvered him securely into her arms so she could twist her way back down into the front seat. As soon as she was pointed forward, she saw what Cullen had so upset. They were coming up on two Jeeps—one of them had men with rifles in their laps. They blocked their progress.

Cullen stopped the truck.

"The two with guns are wearing Rapid Support Forces uniforms," Cullen said quietly in English. Bad news is, we don't know if they're rebels or are with the new government. Let me do the talking."

Carys had already checked her French braid—it was so tight that it was giving her a headache, which meant it wasn't going to show underneath the dark hijab. She brought the scarf down lower over her brow, and the lower part of the robe up higher so that it covered her mouth and nose. Holding Adam should make her blend in as a pious Muslim Sudanese woman. But how in the heck Cullen was going to spin the fact that he was driving her around, she had no idea. She just prayed God that he was a smooth talker.

"Carys, in case the shit hits the fan, here are the keys to the car and a gun." He shoved both at her. She let them drop beside her on the seat. "Now it could be I need you to act as my backup."

"Your backup? What does that mean?" she asked.

"You'll know."

He got out of the truck and went to the first man holding the rifle. He must have recognized the highest-ranking soldier. She heard him say, "Peace be upon you," in Arabic. But then Adam started whimpering and she couldn't hear them.

When the man that Cullen was talking to started screaming, Carys could hear quite clearly. He was accusing Cullen of being a spy. Cullen held up his hands, but not in surrender, she could see it was more in a soothing manner. She rocked Adam more, wishing she could hear what Cullen was saying.

When she could finally get the poor little boy to take a little bit of the bottle, she started to hear talk of money. How come she wasn't surprised? She had hundreds of piasters and Sudanese pounds tucked away in hidden compartments, and on her person, but it always came down to U.S. dollars. She saw Cullen pull out two bills. He was smart, it wasn't as if he took out a wallet and drew out money, or pulled bills off a wad of cash, he just had two rumpled bills from a pocket of his thobe.

Even from her seat, she could see the avarice in the man's eye. He was definitely considering trying to extract more money from Cullen.

"I wouldn't if I were you," Cullen said in a calm tone. Once again Carys was impressed with how well he spoke Arabic.

"I have the gun," the man said. "What are you going to do about it?"

That was her sign. She picked up the gun and put her hand outside the window and trained it on the scene in front of her. There wasn't a chance in the world that she would make the shot, but they wouldn't know it.

"Look over at the truck, you're not the only one with a gun." She would bet anything that Cullen was grinning. All the African men's eyes swung to her.

Please, Adam, don't fuss. Don't fuss.

"Look, I really don't want any trouble," she heard Cullen say. "Let me go back to my truck, I have just a little bit of American money, not much, but a little, that I can give you. But I need more water. Is it a deal?"

Her heart was in her mouth as she waited for their response. Finally, the man motioned with his rifle. Cullen turned and sprinted to the driver's seat. He opened the car door and she saw him duck down, push the thobe out of the way, then fumble underneath his bulletproof vest. He pulled out a bunch of raggedy bills.

She cocked her eyebrow in question. "Later, Carys." He threw all but one of the bills on the car seat and ran back to the men.

"Found it."

The man who didn't have a rifle and wasn't wearing a red beret pulled out a half-full plastic jug of water. He thrust it forward.

"Nope, get down and hand it to me, and I'll trade you the twenty dollars for it. That, and safe passage."

"I'm a man of my word," the leader sounded offended.

"This is a bad situation. It is my task to worry about my woman. I must be careful," Cullen shrugged.

That seemed to get through and the leader told the man with the water to get down and make the trade. All Carys could think about was how heavy the gun was, and how she needed them to hurry up.

"Thank you," Cullen said formally when they concluded their deal.

The leader bowed his head and Cullen did the same. He walked slowly back to the truck. When he got into the driver's seat, he didn't even move the money. He just sat on it, dumped the jug of water at her feet, took the offered keys from Carys, started the truck, and pulled away from them. She saw them staying where they were in the sideview mirror.

"Thank God, my arm was getting ready to drop this thing." Carys started to pull the gun back into the car.

"Stop! You need to keep it trained on them until they're out of sight."

The muscles in her arm were burning, she didn't know if it was physically possible. "Cullen," she started.

"You can do it, I know you can."

"I'm glad you do," she muttered. Her triceps dug deep into the side of the car, her forearm felt like it was going to fall off and the gun trembled in her hand.

"Cullen, I'm going to drop the gun."

"No, you're not. You're Carys Adams, you get the job done no matter what."

"I know who I am," she bit out. "That's why I'm telling you I'm at my limit. Drive faster." She started counting seconds in her head.

"Just one more minute, Carys," he urged. "Almost there, Darlin'. You've got this."

She fought back tears and held on tighter to the pistol. She heard Adam's snuffle over the car's engine, as if he was encouraging her too.

The gun started to slip.

"Done!" Cullen shouted.

She gripped tighter, stopping the fall of the gun, and moved her aching arm back into the car. She deployed the safety and carefully placed the gun next to the jug of water at her feet. The sob of relief took her by surprise. Cullen wrapped his hand underneath her braid and squeezed her neck. It felt wonderful.

"You did good."

She cuddled Adam close to her breast, needing all the intimacy she could get.

"Were they going to shoot us?" she finally asked.

"I'm not sure," Cullen said. "I'm still not sure that they won't follow us even though they were initially going in the other direction. The only thing that gives me hope is that it looked like they were in a hurry to go the other way."

"Where do you think they were going?"

"My guess is Alshbarga. Kane said that there is a build-up going on down there."

She nodded, too tired to do much else, but still, she looked over the seat to check on Shada. Her ebony skin had taken on a pallor that did not look good. "Cullen, when can we stop?"

"I need to put a few more kilometers between them and us before I feel good about stopping."

"We could just end up running into someone else. We need to stop. I need to check her vitals and make sure the saline is still getting to her. She doesn't look good. Can't you pull off into the trees?"

Cullen looked over at her, she could see the determination on his face.

"As soon as I see a good spot, I'll pull off," he promised her.

"Thank you."

Carys sank back against the seat. Little Adam gave a whimper. His wet diaper had soaked into the fabric of the hijab while she'd been holding the gun. Even when she changed him, the scent of urine would still permeate the air around her. The relief she felt at the fact that he was hydrated enough to pee through his diaper and cause such a wet stain on her hijab thrilled her.

Carys smiled and pressed her face into Adam's neck. "You're such a good boy, I love you so much."

"You sure did a number on this diaper, didn't you?" Cullen grimaced. Who would have thought this mission would have called for him to be changing diapers with psychedelic African patterns? Carys had used the children's bedspread to make up additional diapers for the trip. Cullen used some of the precious water to ensure that Adam was thoroughly cleaned up.

He missed Pampers and Wet-Ones, he just thanked his lucky stars that there were two safety pins to use. He carefully pinned the cloth. He wished Carys, with her small, delicate fingers, was performing the task, but she was caring for Shada.

He put his face close to Adam's, watching as the little guy attempted to focus. "You ready to get going again? We're going on an adventure, but first, we must call one of your uncles. What do you think, will Uncle Raiden answer this time?"

He picked him up and rocked him in the crook of his arm like a football as he pulled out his satellite phone.

"We have a big problem," without any preamble.

"What?"

"I have one traumatized little girl."

"What the hell are you talking about?" Cullen's blood pressure rose. "You better not be talking about Aamira or Leila."

"It's Leila," Raiden confirmed. "A man dressed as an orderly at the hospital was caught trying to take her. He got as far as the parking lot before one of the nurses raised enough of a commotion that we got her. It turns out that he was working with the rebel forces."

"I don't get it, why in the hell would they be interested in Leila?"

"She said that her dad was a rebel soldier, but when

Kane and I got her to describe his uniform, we realized that he's not just a foot soldier, he's a fucking major. We've got a real problem. He's going to be after his family."

"What about his wife? Does he know that she's not at the hospital in Khartoum?"

"Yeah, Leila told the phony orderly that she was left behind with you and Carys. Now that they know we're going to be protecting the kids here, I don't think they're going to make another attempt. But you? Yeah, they're going to be coming after you with guns blazing."

"Fuck! Carys was already on their most wanted list, this just makes the stakes that much higher."

"The good news is that maybe they'll try to take you alive."

Cullen thought about Carys' dream and shuddered. She wouldn't think alive was better if he had to guess.

"They're not going to get a shot at Carys or Shada." Cullen's voice was deadly. Adam started crying. It had to have been Cullen's harsh words. Cullen shoved the phone up between his ear and shoulder, then started to stroke his finger down the baby's forehead to the tip of his nose again and again. Then the little stinker opened his mouth like a fish.

"Are you listening?"

Cullen didn't trust that his finger was clean enough, so he just kept stroking the little boy's face.

"I'm listening. I'm listening. How long ago was this?"

"Only two hours ago," Raiden said. "It would take three and a half to get to their house. How far have you gotten from there? You've been driving for five or six hours now, right?"

"Shit, Raiden, we've only gotten twenty kilometers, tops. We've had to go slow so that Shada's incision doesn't open up."

"Hold on."

There was a hell of a long pause. Cullen peeked around the bed of the truck and saw that both doors of the back passenger seat were closed. Carys must be done administering to Shada. He didn't find her in the front seat, where had she gone?

He opened his mouth to call for her, then shut it. He'd just gotten the little guy calmed down. He saw her footprints in the red clay. She'd gone deeper into the trees. Maybe it was a call of nature. He'd give her sixty seconds, then he was tracking her pretty ass down.

He said the numbers out loud in a sing-song voice, figuring it would continue to soothe the little guy since he was still puckering up like he needed food. When he said number fifty-eight, Carys came out of the trees no longer wearing her tan hijab.

"You're this close to being court-martialed," Cullen said as he held his fingers close together.

"What's the charge?"

"You're out of uniform and you were missing in action."

She held up the long robe. "I rinsed out the baby pee. The smell was going to end up suffocating us as the day heats up even more, and I needed a potty break myself. Am I still in trouble?"

"Yes," he said seriously. "Let me know when you're going to leave."

"You were on the phone, I didn't want to interrupt."

"Carys, you interrupt. Never walk off without informing me. I'll give you the same courtesy. Our situation is too volatile." He said it all with a smile in his voice, but he could see that Carys got the fact that he wasn't a happy camper.

She bit her lip and nodded. "You got it. I would definitely feel the same way in your position. I guess I wasn't thinking."

Cullen shook his head. "Shit, with everything you've been through, you've been wonderful. I didn't mean to be an ass."

Carys grinned and the dimple he was so fond of peeped out on her right cheek. "Uhm, something tells me if you weren't holding a baby I would have gotten royally chewed out, you were fine."

He shrugged in agreement. "Speaking of babies, this one is going to start crying for his bottle pretty soon."

"We need some way to heat up the water for the formula."

"Since we're dealing with a glass bottle and a twenty-year-old vehicle, we can work this out. Let's get a move on. Then you can tell me how our patient is doing."

She sighed. "Is there any way we can wait just a little longer so she can rest more?"

"No. We have issues. Get into the truck and I'll show you how we're going to warm up Bubba's bottle."

"What kind of issues?" she turned toward the truck. She was fast, she had the bottle at the ready and her arms out to receive Adam by the time he got to her side of the vehicle.

"Hop in and I'll tell you."

9

"Clever," Carys said when Cullen handed her the cigarette lighter. "I forgot cars had these." It was awkward to hold it underneath the glass bottle and hold onto Adam, but she managed it. After the water was heated, she put in the powder and shook up the mixture.

Finally, as if he knew his dinner was close, he let out a lusty cry.

"My baby," Shada said weakly from the back. "What is wrong?"

"He's just hungry," Cullen assured her in Arabic. "Dr. Adams is getting his bottle ready right now. How are you feeling, ma'am?"

"I'm fine, sir."

Carys heard the fear and deference in Shada's voice and she was torn between sorrow and anger. But before she could follow that bunny trail of emotion, Adam's squalls got louder, demanding all her attention.

"Please, Doctor, I am better, may I hold my son?"

Carys closed her eyes. Shada wasn't doing better. She needed to rest. Carys had administered another small dose of painkiller, but she heard the longing in the woman's voice, and what's more, she knew that the bonding between mother and child was extremely important.

"Yes, Shada. Let me make sure his formula isn't too hot." She needed to do one thing at a time. She looked over at Cullen. She was so tired—she couldn't understand how he was holding up as well as he was. As if he could feel her eyes on him, he glanced over at her.

"Is it cool enough now?"

Shoot, she hadn't been paying attention. She tested some milk on the inside of her wrist. It was warm, but not too warm.

"Give the bottle to me," he said. "I'll hold it while you give Adam to his mom."

She nodded and undid her seatbelt and got up on her knees, leaned over the front seat and placed the baby in Shada's shaky arms.

"Do you have him? You don't have to do this."

Carys hadn't even finished the sentence before mother and baby were cuddled together. Carys leaned even closer. "Shada, open your robe and let Adam nestle against your chest. It's good for him to feel your skin and hear your heartbeat, okay?"

She saw the woman's eyes flicker up to the back of Cullen's head.

"He is an honorable man, he will not look for the brief moment that it takes you to do this small thing."

Shada nodded and moved her clothing so that Adam was soon skin to skin. Even before he got his bottle, he immediately settled. Shada's smile was breathtaking. The bruising on her face was still horrid though. Who would have beat up a woman who was nine-months pregnant? He had to be a monster.

"My son, I am here for you," Shada murmured as she kissed the top of his head.

Carys thrust her hand toward Cullen and he placed the bottle into it. She handed it to Shada, who then started to feed her hungry baby.

"Carys, sit your cute tushie back down and put on your seatbelt," Cullen growled in English.

For once, Shada didn't even flinch at Cullen's less than soft tone. But he better darn well not pull that again. Carys sat her tushie down and made sure they were on a straightaway. When she felt secure on where they were driving, she hit Cullen in the shoulder.

"What the hell was that for?" he sputtered.

"She gets scared at any man's angry tone of voice. So, keep it calm."

"But you are abusing me and acting like a drill sergeant is okay?"

Carys looked over her shoulder. Shada's eyes were wide with amazement. "I think I'm being a good role model for her."

"Great, she's going to think that American men are pussy-whipped," Cullen sighed. But Carys couldn't help but notice that he was holding back a grin.

"You promised to tell me why there is a target on our back."

"Leila's all right," he started.

Carys' throat clenched. She didn't like how this was starting. She sucked in air in a small sip, then blew it out. He'd said she was fine. That was the important thing.

"Okay. She's good. Got it. What happened?"

"One of the rebel forces got to her. Raiden figured out that her dad is high up with the rebels. Somehow, they got word that his family was taken to the hospital by Americans. They tried to take her, but a nurse caused an uproar, so Leila got away, but not before she gave him some information about us."

"How high up?"

"All Leila could do was describe his uniform and tell my team how people referred to him. By the sounds of it, he's the right hand to the colonel of the rebel Rapid Support Forces. That's the man who used to report up to one of the many generals that have been in power. Who knows which one that is these days. The colonel is still out there coordinating things."

"What's the father's name?"

"Kafeel Mubarek. He and the Colonel are both wanted for war crimes. It's bad stuff, Carys."

"Hell, all I have to do is look at what he's done to his wife and children to know what the bastard is capable of," she said bitterly. "How does Raiden think he'll be able to find us?"

"One good thing is that the RSF isn't using helos, so we're good that way. But they have some fast trucks and Jeeps. He expects that they are close to his house now. The one thing we have going for us is that we didn't go the way they expected. They will have thought that we went the straight way back to Khartoum. Instead, we headed east."

"And here I'd been thinking you were nuts."

His head swiveled. "Really?"

She smiled. "No. I figured whatever you were doing must be the right thing. I trust you implicitly to keep us safe."

"Good, because I've got more bad news." He again glanced over at her, gauging her response. When he saw her nod, Cullen blew out a stream of air through his teeth. "You and your team have been targeted by the RSF—they're trying to make the new prime minister look bad."

"How do you know we've been targeted? Are you sure?"

He didn't say anything as he avoided a huge pothole.

"Cullen, are you sure?" They were speaking in English, but her worry must have come through because Shada asked if everything was okay.

"Yes, Shada," Carys assured her in Arabic. "He's telling me about some friends. Everything is fine." She gripped her fingers together until the knuckles were white. "Has something happened?" she asked in English. She kept her voice even.

"Look, I don't have names, but things got out of hand. I just know that some of the people involved with the Doctors Without Borders contingent have been killed."

Her hand shot out and she gripped his thigh. Her nails dug in. "How many?"

"Four." He hesitated. "But two more are missing. The C.I.A. found your name, I'm assuming with some others, on a list that they got from the rebels."

"I don't care about that," Carys tried to keep the tears and anguish out of her voice so as not to upset Shada. "I care about my friends. Were they Americans?"

"I don't know."

"You need to stop the truck."

"No Carys, I really don't."

"Yes, you do. I need to get to my phone, and it's in my backpack in the bed of the truck. I need to find out who was killed. I have to talk to Jamal."

"You're not getting it, Carys. Those men we just left behind could have called to someone else. We could still be in the shit. As long as we're on this road, we are not stopping for any reason."

Her stomach clenched. Dead was one thing, missing was something else entirely. She didn't think she could ever handle that again.

As if he read her mind, he picked her hand up off his thigh. "You said you trusted me implicitly, is that true?"

"There are situations that are too much for anyone."

"Carys, I might have told them that you were the one with the gun, but that was just a diversionary tactic. It was the way to get out of there with the least amount of suspicion. I could have killed them just as easily."

He squeezed her hand, then she felt his thumb

caressing her palm. "Hell, I could have taken them out even more easily than how we handled it," he grinned. "But all that gunfire would have scared the hell out of Shada, wouldn't it?"

"Yes."

"There you go. I'm not going to let anything happen to you. You can take that to the bank."

Carys felt herself relax. But she couldn't stop the tears as she thought about her friends who had died or were missing.

~

He was not happy. Not happy at all. He had done exactly what Kane had told him and so far they'd passed next to nothing and now he was using one of the precious cans of fuel. It was time for Kane to pull a fucking rabbit out of his ass.

"Do you have me located?" he growled at his friend before he had a chance to greet him on the phone.

"No, I was busy evacuating personnel instead of taking a pleasure drive through the country with a beautiful woman," Kane gritted out.

What the hell?

"What the hell are you talking about?" Cullen demanded.

"A bomb went off at the embassy. Two marines were killed. We still have over two hundred Americans who haven't made it out of here, and six are high-value targets."

"Ah, shit." Cullen pictured the fresh-faced new

Marine recruits excited at their first big assignment. He shut his eyes, then turned it off. "Kane, what went wrong? Does this have anything to do with the medical personnel that were targeted? And why in the hell are high-value targets still there? I thought you and Max would have had that shit shut down and them evac'd out hours after Raiden and I hit the road."

"Ah, hell, Cullen. The sad part is, I kind of get it." Kane sounded tired. "They're all in the state department, including the ambassador who's been trying to help Prime Minister Hamdok. He just got his country off the terrorist watch list, our people were attempting to show solidarity with his new regime."

"Dammit, Kane, you're suckering into the do-gooders. That's unlike you. Stop it! Knock them over the head and get them the hell out of there."

In his mind's eye, he could see Kane raking his hand through his short hair. Sometimes his friend needed to be saved from himself. So did Max for that matter. This was Cullen's job; if somebody was going right, he'd pull them left. He always played devil's advocate to keep his friends safe, even if he disagreed with his own thoughts on the situation, because when it came down to it, the only thing that really mattered was keeping his brothers alive. He didn't give a shit if people thought he was argumentative half the time, he just kept his people safe.

"Cullen, give us some credit, will you? We're not just following their lead. I was just saying I could understand their position. The real problem is—"

"The airport's closed." They said simultaneously.

"Don't tell me there isn't a back-up plan. What is it?" Cullen demanded.

"Two Ospreys are being flown in from the carrier that's parked out in the Red Sea."

"That will take care of some of the people, what about the rest?"

"Some will go out with the high-value targets, but the rest will go out on a flight from the Khartoum airport to Egypt. The Ospreys will be dropping off thirty pissed-off Marines. They'll protect the airport." Cullen heard Kane's blood-thirsty grin through his satellite phone.

"Okay, now I get why you're in a shit-ass mood, but now back to what matters, which is *my* problems."

Kane laughed, which is the reaction Cullen had been aiming for.

"Yeah, well while you've been on the phone, I grabbed the comp, and got your phone signal and zeroed in on your coordinates. I figured you're low on fuel and I see you're in the middle of nowhere."

"Gee thanks, Dad. Like I haven't figured that out."

"Well, Dad's here to help."

God, I hope so.

Carys had all four doors of the truck open so that Shada could get some fresh air. She'd also climbed in to do more of a thorough check on her abdomen. He'd offered to hold Adam, but now that Shada was alert she was reticent about having the strange man holding her child.

"How sturdy is the truck you're in? And I mean how sturdy? Can you go four-wheeling?" Kane asked.

"Oh, hell yeah, it's one of them there Unimogs."

"Well, shit, boy, you could climb Mt. Everest in that thing."

"The problem is my cargo. Carys has been clear—I can't be rocking her patient around."

"You don't have much of a choice, man. I need you to go east, totally off-roading, then circle back towards civilization. It's the only way to keep you off the bad-guys radar but get you someplace where you can get some petrol. You need to determine how many klicks you can make on the turn based on the fuel you have— just go far enough that you're out of sight. I've got the satellite imagery right here in front of me. You're not dealing with any big obstructions, but just a lot of rough driving. Since the truck has the clearance and isn't a total piece of shit, then I can get you three klicks outside of Wad Gala.

"You don't want to drive into the city, they'll be looking for you. You're going to have to do your thing, Subterfuge Man. Somehow, you're going to have to circumvent that city and get over to the main highway that will take you directly into Khartoum without having any of the rebels spotting you and pulling you over. It's simple."

"I want a new father," Cullen whined.

Kane didn't say anything for so long Cullen almost wondered if he'd lost the connection, but he knew his friend; he was just letting him digest all the shitty news he'd just laid on him.

"I'm good with everything but the four-wheeling adventure. I think Shada could end up dying, Kane."

"Talk to Dr. Adams. I'm betting she might end up in bad shape, but if she can survive, she can be cared for when she arrives in Khartoum. If you're caught out there with your dick waving in the wind doing nothing, she's dead for sure."

Cullen closed his eyes. Kane was right. That's what he got paid for, making the hard decisions.

"Help me out, Kane, give me the longitude and latitude of where I'm heading."

"I'm sending it through to your phone right now."

"Carys," Cullen called from the front of the truck. He was always careful to make sure that Shada couldn't see him. He wanted to protect her modesty in this situation as best as he could. Carys backed out of the back seat and Cullen couldn't even work up the energy to admire how her butt looked as she wiggled backward. She took one look at his face and turned back to Shada.

"I don't want Adam to get too much sun, I'm going to shut the back doors, okay?"

The woman must have nodded, because Carys went and shut both back doors. She then joined him at a slow pace. She knew that he didn't have good news.

"Just give it to me straight, I'm already imagining the worst."

"We don't have enough gas to make it to the next town by this road. The only way we're going to make it is if we cut across through the trees out toward the desert. The area through the trees is going to be really rough, it's not going to be as bad through the desert, but I'm not going to lie to you, that will be rocky as hell without some kind of path or road."

"And this is the best decision possible, Cullen?"

"It's the only decision."

Cullen watched as Carys took a slow breath and shut her eyes. Then she opened them. This time, her eyes looked bottle green, as if they were powered by steel.

"Okay. Let me set some things up in the back seat. We are down to my last bag of saline, so we need to get our butts to a real hospital quickly, so I'm determined to look at this as a good thing."

It was then that it really hit home that Carys was a doctor, a woman with a will of iron who made life and death decisions. She would have made a damn fine SEAL.

"Carys, about Adam," he started.

"I know, he needs to keep up with us. Shada isn't going to be in any shape to take care of him back there. I'm going to have to make sure she's comfortable with pain meds, and what's more I'm going to have to make sure she doesn't move around much, so I'm going to swaddle her down as much as possible."

"You mean tie her down?"

She shrugged.

"I think I can rig something up with the seatbelts back there."

Carys shook her head. "Wait until I administer the morphine, then see what you can do."

He gritted his teeth and nodded. Somehow, she

caught onto how he was feeling—how, he'd never know.

"Cullen. This isn't your fault. However, this works out, you've been our hero."

He snorted.

"Serious to God. You have gotten us further than we should have gotten. And I know, deep down inside, you're the only man in this world who has a chance to get us safely to Khartoum."

"Thanks for the pressure, Babe."

"I can't help but notice your huge grin. I know SEALs, you thrive under pressure."

His gaze narrowed. "Just what SEALs do you know, and how well do you know them?"

"Get us to the next town and I'll dole out more information. How's that for incentive?"

She looked tired. Beautiful, but tired, and there she was trying to make him feel better about a freakin' lousy situation. God love her. He cupped the side of her face and smiled. "I'm going to be looking forward to something a little more substantial than just a story."

He watched in fascination as a blush creeped up her throat to suffuse her face.

"Carys, I know you're going to ensure Shada and Adam are taken care of, but scrounge through my pack, make sure you grab some food for yourself and stay hydrated."

She nodded. "I'll get some for you too."

Of course, she would.

10

"How many Christmas carols do you know?" Cullen asked her.

"Six, just these six, and they don't seem to be working anymore, he keeps crying."

"Okay, it's my turn."

She gave him the side eye. She'd been around enough soldiers and she didn't think that AC/DC was really going to soothe the baby. But maybe she'd get lucky and he would be into country, and let's face it, she was sick of hearing her own voice and Christmas carols. One day she would have to listen to the radio.

When Cullen started the first bar of the old song *Summertime,* she thought she was falling into a bucket of honey. Adam stopped mid-cry, he was just as enthralled as she was. When the song got to the part where it was 'hush little baby don't you cry', Carys would have sworn that Adam smiled, but she knew better, it was gas. Still, it was a nice thought.

Cullen continued to sing in his deep baritone, the

only jarring note was talking about daddy and mommy watching over him, and there wasn't anything good about Adam's daddy. But still, Cullen was watching over him right now, and that was good.

As Cullen finished with the last notes of the song, little Adam's eyes drifted shut.

"You did it," she whispered. "He's asleep."

"Yeah, that sounds about right," Cullen laughed softly. "I try to entertain someone and I end up putting them to sleep."

She chuckled. In her opinion there wasn't anything about Cullen Lyons that bored her.

"I've had some shut eye over the last few forty-eight hours, you haven't. Do you want me to drive for a while? I've been four-wheeling, and driven snow mobiles in Montana."

His head turned slowly toward her, his lips pursed. "Well thank you, ma'am," he said in a Southern drawl. "That'd be a, 'no'."

"And here I was just thinking to myself how much I was liking you. I guess that just went up in a puff of smoke."

Carys couldn't decide if Cullen's burst of laughter made her angry or tickled her because he sounded so darn sexy.

She sighed. It had been worth a try, but she'd known the answer before she'd asked.

SEAL's!

~

"Doc, I thought you were busy crusading around the world, when did you have time to snowmobile in Montana?"

She sighed. "It was with Peter. He and Alex tried to get me to go skiing, but I just didn't see the appeal. However, after driving through Cambodia, I was definitely willing to give it a try."

Why in the hell had he just assumed she was single? Why hadn't they discussed their status?

"Who is Peter? When was this?"

Shit, was she even interested in him? She hadn't asked him if he had a girlfriend.

Fuck me, am I totally misreading this whole situation?

"Peter is a reconstructive surgeon that I worked with in Haiti. He does everything, but he volunteers at least two weeks a year going around the world fixing cleft palates."

"That's very noble." He wondered just how much money a reconstructive surgeon made. He probably had a mansion in Montana.

"I wouldn't call it noble. He's another man a lot like you. However, unlike you, he knows I'm capable of driving a vehicle, and would also know that he isn't Superman, and would get some shut-eye while I took a turn driving."

Cullen couldn't stop himself from laughing.

"Lady, you're a surgeon, this guy is a surgeon, I'm a SEAL. I'm thinking every single one of us has a big enough sense of self and our capabilities that we would know how far we could push in order to get a job done. If I didn't know I could make it safely to Wad Gala, I would be pulling over...to rest. I am not finding fault with your abilities, Carys, I'm not. But, would you let me loose in the operating room if you were tired? Hell no. Same goes. Driving and watching out for the three of you is my job, and I'm damn good at it."

"SEALs."

"And that's another thing, just how many SEALs do you know? And how close are you to Peter? Are you seeing anyone?"

Did all of that just come out of my mouth?

Her laugh might sound like liquid sunshine, but he really didn't appreciate it being aimed at him. Cullen waited.

"Seriously, you can stop laughing at any point now, Carys," he grumbled.

"Come on, Cullen, besides listening to you sing this has been the only thing that has lifted my spirits since we've started on this bumpy trip."

He heard the worry in her voice. She unclipped her seatbelt and, holding the baby close to her with one hand, she reached over the seat to touch Shada.

"How's she doing?" he asked.

"She's breathing okay, which is the best I can hope for right now."

"Then buckle back in." He knew his voice was rough, but he hated it when she wasn't securely fastened. "Then answer my damned questions." He snarled the last part on purpose knowing it would make her giggle again...and it did.

"I know a lot of SEALs. I've been to a couple of barbeques down in San Diego with a team called Black

Dawn. It's been a couple of years since the last time I went, but I've gone. On that team there are two men, Jack Preston and Aiden O'Malley. Both have invited me to their homes when I've been stateside. Now before you get all growly again, they are both happily married men, and I consider their wives friends of mine."

"And the paragon otherwise known as Peter?"

"I think you're saying you like me." He heard the smallest amount of wonder in her voice. Was she kidding? Had she been living under a rock?

"Not only do I like you, I would definitely be handing notes to you in class. I would also be kicking Peter's ass to the curb. Now tell me who he is to you."

"First, you tell me if you've got someone special in your life, and I'll answer your game of twenty questions."

He really liked that question. A lot.

Adam snuffled and she pressed her nose to his neck and crooned to him. Silent Night again. Seriously, the woman couldn't carry a tune.

"No, Carys, not seeing anyone. Haven't for a while. I'm finding I'm getting particular in my old age."

She continued to rock the baby, but she looked at him sideways. "Old age my Aunt Fanny. We already agreed you're young."

"Not in SEAL years. I'm old. I'm also betting I've got you beat relationship-wise. Who's Peter?"

"Peter and his husband Alex have been happily married for six years, you have nothing to worry about. I'm not sure you have me beaten on the relationship front. I've been married and divorced, what about you?"

She really didn't play the boy-girl games well. She led with her heart, she played at a deeper level than most of the women he knew. He'd bet his bottom dollar that she married and divorced young and had been gun shy ever since.

He wished he could hold her hand, but the road was too rough.

"When were you married? How old were you?"

"Cullen." Her tone was snippy. He guessed she used that tone when she was talking to newbies at the hospital. "The rules were that you were going to answer some of my questions."

"Yes, ma'am." He smothered a smile when she frowned at him. "Never been married, never been engaged, nor have I lived with a woman. I'm not afraid of commitment. My dad saw my mom one day when he was at the garden center in Akron—she didn't know a perennial from an annual and she was driving the teenage clerk up a wall. Dad fell for her like a ton of bricks, or as he tells it, a bag of sod. Mom took a little longer to warm up."

"So, you're looking for a relationship like your parents?"

"Yep. Kids, pets, laughter, and a love that never stops. Our house will be Grand Central Station for the neighborhood."

"And how do you see this working with you gone all the time?"

"Totally depends on my wife and what we figure out. What's her career like? What are her priorities? I'm not going to do Spec Ops forever, this is a young man's game, and I've been recruited for a desk job. Or I might retire. All I know is that my family is going to come first. That's how it was for my parents, and that's what I want as my kids start growing up. I don't want them saying I wasn't at their soccer games.

"So, do I get to ask more questions? Did I pass?" he asked.

She was silent for a long moment.

"I think I might need to take a bit of a rest. When we stop at Wad Gala, I'm going to need to really examine Shada. Even with her restrained, this rough ride hasn't been good for her."

Cullen spared a glance from the rough terrain to Carys. She looked pale. She could say what she wanted about needing to rest up, but he knew what the problem was. It was his big fucking mouth. But to hell with it. He'd never been this drawn to a woman, and he'd be damned if he wasn't going to put his cards on the table. He was planning on coming out of this alive, and maybe, just maybe, she was someone he could explore a future with.

She gave a big ole fake yawn, then gave him a fake smile. "I'm just going to rest my eyes for a bit." She made sure the sling holding Adam was secure, then she leaned back and pretended to sleep.

Lyons, ever hear of subtlety?

~

"Wake up. We're getting close to the city," Cullen said quietly.

Carys sat up and wondered how she'd slept through the smell of Adam's bowel movement. The boy sure could stink up a diaper.

Cullen chuckled softly. "You should see your expression. Adam let loose an hour ago, but you just slept on through. I was amazed."

She immediately put her lips to the baby's forehead and was not happy. He felt hot. She checked his fontanels, to see if he was dehydrated. She saw Cullen looking at her curiously.

"I'm checking his soft-spots, where the bones on his skull still haven't fused. If they're a little sunken in, he's dehydrated."

"Is he?" Cullen was worried.

"A little. Honey?" She shifted his little body back and forth and his eyes slowly opened. Too slowly. "There's my boy."

"Oh shit, I should have realized Bubba would have been hollering. I screwed up." Cullen smacked the steering wheel.

Adam jolted at the loud noise and his little face screwed up in protest and he let out a cry. Carys smiled. He struggled in his swaddling and she unwound him so that he could move his tiny little fists. She sighed in relief. Anger was good. Very good.

"Are you going to stop soon?" she asked Cullen.

"Just looking for a good place," he said.

She looked around and realized they were out of the desert and back amongst some trees. Off in the distance she saw lights indicating a city. "Is that Wad Gala?"

Cullen nodded as he parked the truck and turned it off.

"How far are we from Khartoum?"

"About a hundred kilometers."

She unbuckled her seatbelt. "You need to change Adam, I've got to check on his mom. She and I are going for a potty break," Carys sighed.

He put out his arms, "You got it. Come here, Bubba. Uncle Cullen wants to see what kind of present you got for him. I'm betting it's messy, foul and green. You could be a cook for the Navy, now couldn't you?"

Shada should have been awake by now. Adam definitely felt feverish. She was out the passenger door and opening the door to the back before she had a chance to process Cullen's words. Laughter was bubbling up when she deftly unstrapped Shada. The man was just a little too enticing for her piece of mind.

Seriously? Enticing? Don't go there. He just talked about his parent's marriage.

Be cautious. Be wary. Heck. Be scared.

She looked at Shada's swollen face and thought about her husband.

Bastard. She might be a doctor, but she wanted to kill him.

Then she thought about Cullen again. Okay, how could she be scared?

Admit it, you're enticed.

She looked back down at Shada.

"Are you with me?" she asked. "Shada?"

She looked around and saw that once again Cullen was changing Adam's diaper on the tailgate of the truck, so she took the time to examine her patient's incision.

She sucked in a deep breath as she pulled away the bloody bandage.

"Ahhhhhh," Shada wailed.

"I know, little Mama," Carys said soothingly in Arabic. "I need to examine you. You have been so brave. You are such a good mother to your children."

"It hurts, Doctor," Shada moaned through gritted teeth. "Am I going to die?"

"Absolutely not. You are going to be alive to see your son's children."

Carys looked at the woman's inflamed incision. The only good thing was that her abdomen wasn't swollen. She dug into the makeshift medical kit and pulled out the blood pressure cuff and stethoscope. When she took her vitals, it confirmed what she'd been thinking, the woman was in bad shape. Bad. Shape. Along with the morphine, she'd been administering strong antibiotics, but in this crap environment, of course the surgical sight was infected, heck, for all she knew it could be chorioamnionitis, but without a lab to test, she was totally in the dark.

"Doctor," Shada grabbed her hand, her grip surprisingly tight. "If I die you must get my children to my mother's uncle. I wrote down his name and gave it to Leila. She will be able to explain to him who I was. I am begging you, will you give me your word that you will take them to Egypt? Their father is evil. Please promise me."

"You're not going to die," Carys said fiercely.

"It is in Allah's hands. Please promise me." Tears began to track down her anguished face.

Carys didn't know if this uncle even existed, so she couldn't in good conscience say that she could get the kids to him. So she promised what she could.

"I will protect your children, Shada."

"You are a good woman."

"Not so good, because I am about to make you take a walk." Carys smiled gently.

"I get to relieve myself?" Shada said hopefully.

"Yes, but this will be painful. It would be easier if we could have Mr. Lyons assist you, just to get in and out of the truck, that is all."

Shada bit her lip, her discomfort was clear. "Is he a married man?" she asked.

Carys abhorred lying, but she considered it so that Shada would feel more comfortable, but she couldn't do it. "No, he is a bachelor, but he is an honorable man. He is a leader and he has been very good with your son."

Shada started to shake her head, but before she could say anything, Carys interrupted her. "Right now, he is once again changing your son's diaper, and he will probably start singing to him again so he will go to sleep."

"He has sung to my son?"

"Yes," Carys nodded.

"Okay, I will allow him to help me."

Carys smiled. "I will see if he is done cleaning up Adam." She left the backseat and went around to the truck bed where Cullen was holding Adam on his shoulder.

"I'll put him down in his nest in the front," Cullen said.

"So, you heard?"

He nodded. "How painful is this going to be? As bad as when you're pressing down on her abdomen?"

"About the same. I'm worried about her. She's clammy and her blood pressure is low. The good news is that she is alert."

"She has you as a doctor, it'll be fine."

How could he say that with so much confidence?

Cullen got Adam settled, and Carys made sure that Shada was modestly covered, and that her sandals were on. She groaned as Carys got her sitting in an upright position. Cullen came up behind her.

"Can I be of help? Perhaps I can lift you out of your seat?" he suggested.

Shada tried to push up first, instead of taking his suggestion, and let out a muffled shriek. She sank back down on the mattress. "Yes please, I need some assistance."

Cullen carefully lifted her out of the backseat. "Where do you want me to take her?" he asked Carys. "Over to those trees?"

"No, we are going to have Shada walk between us, she can hold onto our shoulders. You can do that, can't you Honey?" she asked the woman.

She nodded. Cullen looked horrified.

"I can carry her."

"She needs to walk. It's good for her circulation. This is important."

"I'm fine, Mr. Lyons," Shada assured him in a hoarse voice. He set her down, ready to catch her if she crumpled. He held onto her right arm, and Shada wrapped her arm around Carys' shoulders for support. Slowly, very slowly, they made their way to the trees.

"I will go back and see how Adam is doing. You call me when you need me," Cullen said when they finally had Shada leaning against a tree.

"Thank you, Mr. Lyons," she gasped.

"You are welcome, ma'am."

Carys assisted Shada to urinate and was really worried when there was very little output. With all the saline she'd administered, there should have been more output.

Dammit, was Shada bleeding internally?

Carys took a moment to take care of her own personal needs, then she shouted out for Cullen to come help Shada back to the truck.

Cullen was gritting his teeth as he witnessed Shada's silent pain during she walked back. He helped her to settle into the backseat, then went to administer to Adam who was crying as well.

Carys rebandaged Shada and repacked her kits. Then she backed out of the backseat and followed the sounds of Cullen's singing and Adam crying.

"Your friend Kane, does he know if there is a hospital in Wad Gala?"

Cullen was shaking his head before she even

finished her question. "That's out, Carys, I'm so sorry. But we have to wait until we get to Khartoum."

"We don't have the time to wait. Her blood pressure is dropping. I've run out of saline. I need to get her help."

"If we're spotted, we're done for. We can't risk it."

"That's not an acceptable answer. We're close to a town, they must have a clinic. I'm in a damned hijab, I'll walk in and buy some saline."

"Yeah, with your green eyes and white skin, that's going to work," Cullen's eyes flashed at her.

"Not everybody is black in Africa."

"I realize that, Dr. Adams. I also realize that we have killers who are on the lookout for us, *you* in particular. You have to remember that a bunch of these people are scared and in the pocket of the RSF. They will put the drop on you. You are not going to be wandering around Wad Gala. Got it?"

The deadlier his voice got, the louder Adam cried. The baby could feel the tension in the air.

"Give me the baby." Carys held out her arms.

"At least if you're holding Adam, I know you're not going off half-cocked." He gently placed the newborn into her arms, stroking his finger along his cheek.

"Let's get something straight right now, Chief Petty Officer, I would never just leave. I already told you I trust you implicitly with our safety. I will always defer to you, but that doesn't mean I'm *not* going to argue with you. But me countermanding your directive is just plain stupid."

He looked at her with a stunned expression on his face. "Did you just say that?"

"Huh?"

"You are a Goddess."

She frowned. "What are you talking about?"

"You are straight up logical. I'm totally taking you home with me when we get out of this mess."

"Cullen Lyons, you are really getting on my last nerve, and we don't have time for this. What are you talking about?"

"My sisters would never be this logical, they would always insist that their way was right, and be thinking of a way to go around me, over me, or under me."

"Well, they need to grow up," she said succinctly. "Now figure out a way for me to get saline, and us to get to Khartoum."

"Abso-fucking-lutely. Your wish is my command."

How could she possibly feel like smiling at a time like this, she wondered as she stared into the bluest eyes known to mankind.

11

*T*hank God the red soccer jersey covered the tight tan pants he was wearing, otherwise it would look like he was advertising his junk. As it was, it was hard to walk in the damn things. So much for easy maneuverability, but it was more important to blend in with the crowd. Cullen meandered through the packed streets of Wad Gala. He was getting stares, besides the fact that he was wearing clothing that was like others in the village.

He ducked down one of the many little side alleys. First things first, he needed to find some saline for Shada, hot foot it back to the truck, and then he could get some fuel from the petrol station he'd seen.

Where the hell was a clinic?

Carys had told him what to look for. Mainly, it would be a line of women holding kids. And just how the hell was he going to talk his way to the front of the line and, talk someone out of at least two bags of saline?

First things first, find the clinic.

He had to squeeze his way out of the end of the alley and avoid stepping in a little stream of sewage. But, after Bubba and his green poop, it wasn't so bad. Cullen looked right, left and forward as he moved out into the bright sun, everything looked normal. So, he was still caught off-guard by the three-and-a-half-foot high child who slapped his leg.

"Mister. I get you anything you want. You pay me."

"How old are you?" Cullen frowned down at the kid, then looked around and saw people milling about. Nobody seemed to think anything was odd about him being accosted by this young entrepreneur.

"I'm six. You lost. I help. Need money up front."

Cullen grinned. He liked this kid.

"How many piasters?"

"I want American dollars." The kid held out his hand as his lower lip jutted out and his eyebrows lowered. Cullen bit his lip as he looked over the little man. He was going to be quite the little enforcer when he grew up.

"One Sudanese pound," Cullen offered. "If I like your help when we're done, two American dollars. But you've got to come through for me."

Suddenly the kid was all smiles. "I can help."

"What's your name?"

"Mohammed." He held out his hand again and Cullen went to shake it. "No, I want my money."

Cullen laughed. "Of course, you do."

Once again, he had some crumpled up bills hidden in his pockets, but this time it took some doing to dig them out of the tight pants. The kid watched the spectacle with interest. Cullen finally handed him his money.

"What you want? Beer?"

Cullen was impressed. Beer was pretty hard to come by, and a six-year-old knew how to procure it?

"No beer, I need to find the clinic."

"You sex sick?"

"No." The kid was unbelievable. "I don't have a sexual disease. But I do need some medicine. Now where's the clinic?"

"Follow me." The kid started running. When Cullen just watched him, he stopped and turned around. "You slow. I want my money. Come quick."

Cullen kept up despite his laughter. Wait until he told the guys about Mohammed.

He kept following the kid to the outskirts of town. Why hadn't he realized that? Of course, the clinic wouldn't be as accepted so it would be farther out, at least in one of the smaller towns like this one. And Carys had called it—there was a line of women and some old men coming out of the clinic. But that didn't stop Mohammed from ducking past everyone, despite their protests.

"Come, come, you must hurry," he said as he motioned for Cullen to follow him inside.

There were many women and children standing and sitting inside. Some of them looked very ill. "Come, come," again the child motioned for him. Cullen shook his head. He'd had enough of pushing his way to the front of the line.

The boy rolled his eyes. He darted back behind a desk to a hallway, perfectly comfortable in the little clinic. Soon he came out with a woman who was holding his hand.

"My nephew informs me that you have a life and death emergency, is this true? Or is he once again exaggerating so that he can make some money?" She seemed to know the boy well, but there were equal parts indulgence and impatience in her voice.

"I never told him that, ma'am," Cullen said deferentially in Arabic.

"Then what is the problem?" she demanded. "I don't have all day."

At least he wasn't totally caught wrong-footed, Carys had given him a bit of a cover story in case he needed one. "I have a patient. He had surgery and now he needs saline."

"What are you talking about?" She looked him up and down. "You're no kind of doctor," she said derisively.

She was tough. "No, ma'am. I'm a driver. I'm driving a private car from Wad Madani to Khartoum for a rich old man who just had surgery on his liver. There is a nurse with him."

"Well, where is he? Let me see him."

"Auntie give him what he needs. He will pay."

She folded her arms over her large bosom and gave Cullen a hard stare. "I need to see your patient. I want to make sure he is doing well."

A smile wouldn't work in this case. "Nurse Adams knew you would feel that way," he said. "She said to tell you that his fever has spiked, and I need to move fast."

"Where are they?" The woman demanded again.

"They are outside of town. We ran out of fuel. Nurse Adams said saline was most important, then I will get fuel and take us to Khartoum."

Mohammed grabbed his aunt's hand. "We must hurry," he pleaded. "We cannot let someone suffer."

The kid was good, he tugged harder at her hand. "Please, we must help him."

She looked at Cullen then back down at her nephew. "I will get it for you. It will cost you two hundred and fifty pounds a bag." He was getting off cheap. Ten dollars.

As soon as his aunt was out of sight, he looked up at Cullen, all business. Mohammed held out his hand. "That will be twenty American dollars."

"What are you talking about? She said ten."

"Finder's fee."

The little grifter. Cullen dug into his tight pants and pulled out his crumpled bills and handed them to the kid.

"I can help you get fuel too," the boy gave a toothy grin.

"I'm sure you can."

12

*C*ullen had left her with a flashlight, and if she opened one of the car doors, she'd have light, but the man had left her too scared to call attention to the vehicle in the dark. Luckily, Adam was sound asleep, so he wasn't making any noise in the black night either.

She'd left him sleeping in the truck. She'd made up quite the little baby bed in the floorboard of the passenger seat. He was tucked in like the proverbial bug in a rug. This left her in the truck bed with the gun ready to take on anybody. She just hoped whoever came by was nothing more than a goatherder and she wouldn't need to use a weapon.

For the twenty-seventh time, she yawned.

Cut it out. You had sleep. You're the last person allowed to be tired on this little venture. The baby, the sick woman and the soldier who hasn't slept in three days all get to be tired. Your butt has to be awake and alert.

No beddy-bye-time for you.

She yawned again. Tears pricked the back of her eyelids, she was so mad at herself. She should be better than this. So much better. Her breath shuddered. How many times had she said that to herself?

"Cut it out, Adams," she whispered fiercely. "You don't have time for this horsepucky."

But seriously, how many people in her life could she possibly disappoint? How many?

She rolled her eyes to the heavens.

She had to be tired if she was replaying *those* old tapes. For God's sake, she was a doctor, she was being considered for chief surgeon at a good-sized hospital! She was not a failure!

Once again, she felt her palms sweating as she held the darn gun, and this time it was cold out.

Please, Cullen, come back.

Please be okay.

Please don't be hurt.

God, she couldn't stand it if anything happened to that man. He was so damned special. He might scare the spit out of her, but he made her want. He made her want so *many* things.

She took a deep calming breath.

Another.

In and out. Slowly. Deeply. She would get through this. She would protect Shada and Adam, that was what she did. She took another deep breath.

Then on the fifth deep breath, she thought she heard a faint sound drifting toward her on the dark African night. Was that singing? She held her breath, trying to make out the sound. No, it wasn't singing, it was humming. She listened more intently. Finally, she could make it out.

It was that song, the one that Cullen had sung.

Summertime.

Her joints loosened and her bones melted as she took comfort in the melody that flowed over her. Cullen was coming. He was telling her that everything was all right.

Trembling, Carys crawled out of the bed of the truck.

She slumped against the cold steel and waited, even though every instinct said to run to him. Still, her job was to stay with the little family and protect them.

Darn it, she'd left the pistol in the bed of the truck. She climbed back onto the bumper and reached over the tailgate.

The wolf whistle took her by surprise. When she almost lost her footing, strong male hands captured her and pulled her back against a hard chest.

"Nice booty, Doctor."

"Shhh, you'll wake up Africa," she admonished as she blushed with pleasure. She'd never once been whistled at in her entire life.

"I was quiet," he whispered into her ear. The warm heat of his breath sent tingles all through her body. She was no longer feeling sorry for herself, that was for darn sure. This man, he had her all tangled up. And she really, really, really truly liked it. She shook her head so that she could get herself together.

Adam.

Shada.

Saline.

"Yep, I got it."

"Did I just say all that out loud?"

Cullen's laugh made her heart sing. "You sure did."

"Even the part about you turning me on?"

"That was my favorite part."

She softly hit her forehead against the side of the truck. He pulled her back against his front. "No hurting my girl." He spun her around and kissed her forehead. She held her breath. Would he do more?

She blinked hard. They didn't have time for this.

"Did you get saline?" she asked.

He squatted next to a huge duffel bag on the ground and opened it up.

"The saline's in there. I need to be careful with it."

"Of course you do, the saline is critical," Carys said.

"I'm talking about the bag. That thing cost me an arm and a leg, it's the finest leather, you know. As a matter of fact, everything on this trip was expensive. I met a pint-sized hustler, I thought he was going to talk me out of my underwear and then sell them back to me."

She squinted down at him. "I didn't think you could fit boxers underneath those pants."

"You've been thinking about what kind of underwear I have on? Fancy that, I've wondered about yours." He said it with a sideways grin as he plucked out the two bags of saline from the orange bag.

How could he rile her up and get things done at the same time?

"Do you need any help?" he asked her as he handed her one of the bags. "Where's Adam?"

He was back to business. Good, she needed that.

"Can you check on him? He's in the front seat. I'll work on Shada. I was in the back of the truck. I was—"

"Taking care of your charges. I know, Carys. You always do what's necessary." This time he wasn't flirting, his smile was filled with admiration for her work ethic. That was something she could understand. She nodded.

"Exactly."

He headed for the front seat and she went back to where she'd left Shada. The last three times she'd checked on the woman, it had been the same thing. She'd been feverish and delirious. Carys couldn't get her to eat or drink anything, not even the applesauce.

Weak with relief, Carys hooked up one of the bags of saline and adjusted the drip up temporarily, so that she could get some of the life-giving fluid into Shada's system as quickly as possible. She situated herself in a pretzel position so that the woman's head rested on her lap. Carys desperately wanted to provide comfort to the young mother. It felt like Greece all over again. She didn't know how she would cope if one member of this little family didn't make it.

She heard the click of the engine.

"You making supper?" Carys asked Cullen.

"Bubba's thinking my little finger has the ability to provide sustenance. He's going to figure out pretty soon that no milk is coming his way, so I'm heating up din-din."

"Can you do all that while holding Adam?"

"Honey, this is one of the easiest assignments I've ever had. I have a doctor on call and a baby to cuddle. Hell, I even scored more formula, saline, food for us, two jerry cans of fuel, and I could have had beer and sex medicine if I wanted it."

"What?" She couldn't have heard right. "What is sex medicine?"

"I have no idea."

"And beer? Maybe in Khartoum, but in that little town?"

"I'm telling you, I met a wheeler-dealer who would have made the guys from Ocean's Eleven look like pikers. This kid hustled me."

"How can you say he hustled you when he delivered?"

"Carys, I bring a couple hundred dollars in American money with me on most assignments. That's about any of us need on a mission, that's over-the-top, really. He ended up getting most of my cash, and I felt fine giving it to him, the little shit."

She giggled. She could hear the admiration in Cullen's voice. Then Adam started to whimper.

"I think he caught on to your ruse."

"Hey, little buddy. Dinner's almost ready. Can you hold out for another sixty seconds?"

A louder cry came out. Carys loved hearing it— there was nothing sadder than a baby who was so malnourished, he couldn't even cry.

"What's next on the agenda?" she asked.

"We eat."

"I know, you're feeding Adam."

"No, I'm talking about you and me. It's nine o'clock. I want us to eat, then we're going to sleep until two. I want us on the road at three a.m. That will put us on the highway to Khartoum two hours before dawn. We'll be less likely to be noticed."

"I don't understand. Won't people notice us then, as opposed to during the day when there are more cars on the highway?"

"Our truck is going to be really suspicious with the windows blocked out in the back. If I thought it would be less suspicious to have them unblocked with Shada lying there, I'd go for it, but we're screwed either way. So, we need to fly under the radar, which means at the witching hour."

Shada began to relax in Carys' lap, and in return, Carys' shoulders slumped in relief. The saline was working. She adjusted the drip down.

"Carys, did you hear me?"

"What?"

"I knew you weren't listening. What's going on back there? Is Shada doing better?"

She heard the worry in Cullen's voice, and that too warmed her heart. The amount of care, concern and actual love that radiated through this little slice of Africa tonight was amazing.

"She's doing better. She's not out of the woods. But with the saline you got, she's going to make it to Khartoum."

"Good, because she came too far for this little guy to be without a mom."

"You sound like that would be the end of the world," Carys said quietly.

"It would be."

Wouldn't that be nice to feel that loved by a parent? She didn't know how that felt. She'd been raised by Rosa, and her mom and dad didn't want her to form too much of an attachment to the housekeeper, but they sure as heck weren't offering much from themselves. She could tell that Cullen's upbringing was just the opposite. His parents gave him the love that Shada was trying to provide to her children. Of course, she wasn't providing any sort of protection, at least not yet.

"You're thinking pretty hard over there. I can hear you. You're going to disturb the scorpions."

"Don't remind me," Carys shuddered. It was the main reason she'd taken watch in the truck bed and not beside the truck. She'd heard too many stories about the increase of scorpion stings along the Blue Nile with all of the mining.

"So, tell me what you're thinking about. Tell me a secret," Cullen coaxed.

She heard a rustle on the other side of the seat, and she peeked over. Cullen had Adam tucked up against his shoulder. He was rocking him and rubbing his back. He was trying to get him to burp. What was it about men and babies? Or was it just this man?

"What secret do you want to know?"

"Carys, if I knew, it wouldn't be a secret." His blue eyes captured hers in the moonlight that shone through the windows.

"I wasn't happy in my marriage."

He snorted. "Uhm, you got divorced. That's kind of easy to figure out."

"I mean really unhappy. I knew it was a mistake when I walked down the aisle unhappy. I did it because I could finally do something to please my parents. Derek wanted me to be the pretty little hostess like my mom, so I was an epic failure all around."

"How old were you?"

"Old enough to know better."

"How old," he insisted.

"Twenty-one."

"Let me guess, a sheltered baby. I bet you went to an all-girls' school for high school."

Her head shot up. "How'd you know that?"

"And what university were you going to? If it was to please Mommy and Daddy, was it Smith or Wellesley?"

"Far too political for my parents' tastes. Nope, Bryn Mawr all the way. What took you down the path of all-girl universities? Your sisters?"

"We'll save my secrets for another night. This is you, Dr. Adams. So, tell me how you rebelled."

They were interrupted by, not a burp, but a belch.

"That's my boy. High five." Carys watched as Cullen pulled Adam's hand out of the swaddling and touched his huge palm against Adam's tiny palm. "I think he's ready for bed again. You gave him a pretty sweet set-up." Cullen chuckled. "He's toast."

"Ya think? I don't know how to break it to you, but he's brand new. A three-day-old baby isn't up for high fives," Carys smirked.

"He's a baby genius. Oh, shit, I forgot to take off my shirt." He looked seriously upset.

"I think you're fine. He just needed to be fed. The way he's swaddled also soothes him and helps him to sleep. We're good."

She saw Cullen relax. "Okay, Little Man, let's put your hand back in here, and get you settled for the night."

"Better check his diaper."

"Already did. He's clean and dry. However, after all that formula I see a diaper change in my future."

"I'll take care of it."

"You're going to be sleeping, Missy."

"No, you are. I've been counting, you're on two-and-a-half days without sleep. That's ridiculous." Carys started to extricate herself from under Shada. She used the sheet to wipe the woman's brow. "You're doing good," she whispered in her ear in Arabic. "Your children need you. Get better."

She stretched as she got out of the car and quietly shut the backseat door. Somehow the stealth ninja warrior was beside her. "How do you do that?"

"What?" he asked with a satisfied smile.

"You know what. You sneak around like a thief in the night."

"I'm quieter than a thief. They train us. Anyway, you were louder than Adam at full roar. It was easy to sneak up on you. Do you need a trip over to the trees before we bed down for the night? I now am the proud owner of half a roll of toilet paper."

She knew that her eyes had to be glowing along

with the saliva that was probably dripping out of her mouth. She was down to the last four tissues from the three packets of Kleenex she'd brought.

Cullen fished out a flashlight and the roll of TP, and took out some clothes. "I'll walk with you."

"You don't have to."

"It's in the SEAL code book. I have to."

"Oh yeah, I forgot." She took the proffered toilet paper and walked beside him as he shined the light close to the ground. He found a large rock for her to do her business. When she was done, she found him back in his normal clothes.

She bit back a laugh. "What?" he demanded.

"I'd really hoped I was going to see Raiden's expression when you showed up in the other pants. He's kind of hard to read, so it would have been good to see his reaction."

He gave her a considering look and laced their fingers together as he guided them back to the truck. "Raiden I could have handled. It would have been my friend Kane and my lieutenant that would have had lasting consequences. Kane would take a picture for his fiancée."

"And that would have been bad how?"

"I don't know. That's the problem, she's positively evil. She's worse than Kane and that's saying something. There would be a cake, a banner, a bronze statue. Something."

Carys shook her head—she didn't believe him. When they got to the truck, she peered in at Adam and Shada and they were both sleeping soundly. She indicated the news to Cullen, who smiled. She watched as he hopped—literally hopped—over the side of the truck just using one hand for balance, and he did it without making a sound.

"Hold on, I'll give you a hand up when I get the bedding situated.

"What bedding? There's no bedding."

"I paid prime dollar to Mohammed. We are kitted out. Now, it's not like we have anything so silly as a pillow."

She watched as he pulled out a Dora the Explorer blanket. "How old did you say Mohammed was?"

"He couldn't have been older than six years old. This blanket was the only thing that seemed kid-like about him. Well, I guess the Spiderman blanket was kind of kid-like, but when I asked for that instead, I couldn't afford it."

She snickered. "So, six? And he was that much of a wheeler-dealer?"

"Yep. He took me around to almost every store and stall in that little town, and every single shop keeper knew him. It was obvious he brought in a bunch of business. Not only was he skimming money from me, he was taking a cut from each of the vendors. That kid had it coming and going."

"You're kidding me."

"Nope."

"Was he being taken advantage of?" She'd seen it before. Kids being used as shills by adults. It was a form of exploitation.

Cullen laughed again. "I checked it out. I met the

whole family. I mean the *whole* family. I swear, he's related to half the town. Not a mark on him. He took me to his house and showed me his collection of comic books. They were his treasures. Nope, he's fine. Part of the reason he targeted me was so he could practice what little English he had. He's determined to be able to read some of those comics by the time he's eight. The kid has *goals*."

Carys grinned. She wished she could go to Wad Gala and meet the boy.

Cullen came to the tailgate and crooked his finger at her. She darn near tripped over her own feet to get there. He hoisted her up into the bed of the truck and she practically swooned at the sight of the blankets.

Heaven.

"Are you going to be okay sleeping next to me?" Cullen asked seriously.

Could the man be any nicer? If she wasn't so tired, she knew she would be shy, embarrassed and more than a little turned on at the thought of lying next to this man.

She stopped short and looked at him in wonder. This would be the first time since the incident in Las Flores that she would be sleeping next to a man, and here she was looking forward to it. Who would have guessed?

"Carys, are you okay?" His voice was husky as he looked down at her. She couldn't form any words. "Carys? Why don't I grab the thobe, and just go sleep out on the ground? It's not a problem."

She clutched at his arm. "Absolutely not. That's not

it at all. I'm fine with us in the truck together. I'm more than fine, and it surprised the heck out of me."

He reached up very slowly and cupped her cheek. "I hadn't thought about what you went through in Los Flores. I just assumed it was so long ago..."

She searched his eyes, begging him to continue.

"When was the last time you slept with a man, Carys?"

"So long. It's been so long. But I'm not scared with you." She swallowed. "To sleep together." She swallowed again. "I mean to sleep in the truck together." Her hand gripped him harder. "I mean—"

His thumb brushed over her lip.

"Honey, I know what you meant. It's all good. Nothing's going to happen tonight but us eating dinner and getting some shut-eye. I'm honored that you feel safe with me."

Her entire body relaxed.

"Thanks for understanding."

He gave her his crooked grin. "Now let me show you what Mohammed wrangled up for us."

Carys was happy to change subjects. She sat down cross-legged on the blanket as he started pulling out things from the duffel. She was happy not to see a protein bar or MRE in the bunch. The warm can of orange Fanta was almost obligatory. Her mouth watered. How many of these had she drank over the years? Two large bottles of water, that were properly sealed and not glued shut. Another can of warm Fanta.

"Pineapple," she eeped. "Mine!"

"We have a fan," he grinned as he handed over the bright yellow can. She held it close to her breast.

"I love pineapple. I don't care what else you have in there. This wins the day."

"Well, we have some flatbread," he said as he pulled out something that looked like tortillas or naan in waxed paper. "Here's some gheema, which is spiced potatoes. He kept trying to offer me his mother's spicy meat. I couldn't pass on it otherwise I would have seemed rude, but I left it out in the desert for one of the critters to eat. The last thing we need is something that's not going to agree with our intestinal tract."

"Been there, done that," Carys agreed. "The last time was goat in Pakistan."

"Yeah, and he never would tell me what type of meat it was. So, this is an all-vegetable and starch dinner."

"And Fanta," she said as she petted her yellow can of soda.

"Oh, and we have dessert." He pulled out a piece of cake that was also wrapped in waxed paper. "His mom served it with some excellent cinnamon tea. I tried to get out of there as quickly as I could, but I was stuck."

"I understand." And she did, you had to be gracious. Especially when someone was helping you as much as the child had been.

"This is lemon cake. It's awesome. So, this piece is for you."

She looked at it longingly. She loved sweets. Even more than chocolate, something fruity like this was her downfall.

"I don't want to take this from you," she demurred.

"Well, now I know the way to your heart," he smiled warmly.

He might make her feel safe, but he also made her feel wanted. She looked down and slowly popped open her can of soda, glad that she had when it started to fizz. Boy, wasn't that a metaphor for her feelings.

"Careful," he whispered.

"I'm not sure I can be," she admitted.

"That's true, you were ogling that drink like it was Christmas and your birthday all rolled into one."

Sure, I'll stick with that answer.

She closed her eyes and took a sip of the pineapple goodness and thanked God it took her mind off Cullen's blue eyes and wide shoulders for a moment.

13

"Carys, I'm going to go out and make another call. I need to check in with my lieutenant. I don't want to disturb our charges."

"Why not make it here?" she asked.

"You know these satellite phones—usually you have to talk loudly or sometimes even yell to be heard."

"There is that. Can you ask again for the names of who was killed and who's missing? Please."

"I can, but I'm betting that it will be the same answer. If Max didn't have the answer last time, they probably aren't likely to have released any names since then."

He saw her open her mouth to protest.

"I promise to ask, I just don't want you to get your hopes up is all."

She bent her head. "I know. It's just when I call, I've only been able to get ahold of Jamal and Hans, and they don't know anything."

He reached out and covered her hand with his.

"We'll be in Khartoum soon. Then you'll know," he assured her.

"Go make your call," she said as she made a shooing motion. He gave a grin and hopped over the side of the truck. That woman was something else. He jogged out a good ways where he thought his voice would at least be muffled. He wanted a good idea of what they would be running into when they got to the capital city and he didn't want to worry Carys unnecessarily.

He called Kane, knowing he'd know exactly what the hell was going on.

"Take this," it was Leo's voice.

"Sato here."

There was a massive roar from a crowd. Kane could barely hear his teammate. "Raiden, it's Cullen. I'm checking in. I'm going to be coming into Khartoum early tomorrow morning. I've got to get Shada to a hospital."

Cullen continued to hear people yelling, but Raiden wasn't saying anything.

"Raiden. Talk to me."

"The main highway into the city is closed off. They're rioting in the streets. There are hospitals open. There have to be with all of the wounded civilians, but I'm trying to think of how to get you to one of them."

"What the fuck are you talking about?" Cullen demanded. "This is not some kind of movie. Khartoum is a city of five million."

"With basically one way for you to get into the city from where you're at," Raiden ground out.

"Who the hell has the highway blocked off? The Rapid Support Forces?"

"Civilians. It's a goatfuck."

Cullen dropped down into a crouch and dropped his head onto his knees. How could they be this close, and end up having it all fall to shit? He took a deep breath and tried to get his tired brain to think. It wasn't working. It wasn't working at all.

"Look, Cullen, I'll talk to Kane. He's over at the airport right now. Midnight Delta has been brought in to help. He's coordinating with them right now. When was the last time you've slept?"

"Doesn't matter," Cullen bit out.

"Yes, it does. You're not worth two shits if you can't think straight. Rely on your team right now. You need to get some rest. When are you planning on getting on the road?"

Cullen looked down at his watch. "I wanted to be on the highway at O-three-hundred hours."

"Okay, sleep for the next five hours, then call me back up. We'll have a plan."

Cullen was silent.

"You've got to trust your team. Haven't we always had your back?"

Cullen relaxed.

"Yeah," he said. "You guys have never let me down."

"Exactly."

∼

By the time he had walked back to the truck, Cullen

had taken his teammate's words to heart. Worrying was stupid at this point, and Raiden was right, his team always came through. What's more, he desperately needed some sleep. When he got to the bed of the truck, he saw Carys setting down her treasured soda to pile some spiced potatoes onto a piece of flatbread.

A strand of her hair had made its way out of her braid and it was now curled around her face. She swiped at it like it was a spider or something. Then she shoved it back into her braid and gave a sigh of relief. There was definitely a story there.

"Well, come sit down and eat and tell me about the call," she motioned for him to join her.

"Let's wait until after dinner, okay?"

"Did you find out about my friends?"

"No, I didn't."

She slumped, then sighed. "Okay, we can wait until after we eat." He watched as she took a delicate bite of her food, thoughtfully chewed, and then smiled. "This is good. I never quite know what I'm going to get. Of course, I always *pretend* it's good. But this, I actually like."

He liked that. Every one of his team members respected the different cultures that they encountered and were always polite and gracious. The fact that Carys was the same way just raised her even higher in his esteem.

"So, it's not just the sweets that you like?" he teased.

She gave a wry smile. "So, I didn't hide my mouth watering over the cake as well as I'd hoped, huh?"

"I thought you might scratch my eyes out if I had

suggested we share."

"Nah, you're a too good of a driver." She said before taking another bite.

He grinned around the large bite of food he had taken. After he swallowed, he asked, "Wanna tell me what other vices you have?"

"Oh no, you asked all the questions last time, soon it will be my turn. But it's doctor's orders that you rest as soon as you brief me on the call."

The woman was right. It was time for shut-eye. She'd been an absolute trooper, but the dark mauve bruising under her eyes was visible even under the quarter moonlight. All the care she had been giving to her two charges had drained her, and no amount of sugar was going to recharge her the way that some rest would.

He settled back against the side of the truck and finished up the rest of his Fanta, then opened up one of the bottles of water and handed it to her.

"Thanks." She took a sip and her hair got in her way again, then she swiped at it angrily.

"Carys? What's wrong?"

"Nothing. I'm just overtired and when I am, I hate it when my hair is in my face."

He reached out slowly and brushed it back behind her ear. Her sigh of relief was audible.

"It's a phobia."

"No big deal. We all have them."

"Now that's two for me. Messy hair and scorpions. At least I don't faint at the sight of blood." Her eyes twinkled.

"Yeah, you'd be kind of a crap doctor if you did." He nudged the piece of cake toward her.

She shook her head. "I'm going to save it for breakfast. I would give it to Shada, but she's still sound asleep and on the off-chance she needs surgery when we get there, I want her stomach empty." She leaned over to her medical kit and pulled out an empty bottle of water. He watched as she poured the rest of her soda into the empty water bottle and capped it.

"What are you doing?"

"I'm going to give this to Shada when she wakes up. This will be *her* treat for breakfast." Then she leaned forward and broke off a corner of the cake. "Okay, Mama needs a little taste before bedtime."

Cullen was grateful for the fact that he was wearing a looser pair of pants. God, the woman looked like she was in the throes of ecstasy.

Down, boy.

They yawned at the same time.

"I'm too tired to say jinx," she yawned again. "Can you tell me what was said on the call?"

"There's rioting in the streets going on. The highway going into the city is closed off."

She gasped.

"But the good news is that they've brought in another SEAL team. This is going to work out."

"It is?"

"It is," he promised her. "Kane and Raiden are working on a plan while we rest. They'll have something for us by the time we wake up."

"But—"

"Sometimes there's nothing you can do for a patient but wait and see, right?"

"Yes," she admitted. "Those are the times I hate the most."

"You and me both. But I trust my teammates implicitly. You and I both need rest so we can pull off whatever they have planned for us. Okay?"

She stared at him, her eyes searching his face for something. He didn't know what, but she must have found it, because she said, "Okay, Cullen. You're right. We need to sleep."

He pulled back the Dora blanket and showed her the plaid blanket that was folded for padding underneath.

"Settle in," he invited. "You're going to have to make do with the empty duffel bag as our pillow."

"*We* are," she corrected. She was lying down and looking up at him when she said it. "Seriously, Cullen, just get in here. I'm cold, and we're sharing the darn pillow." With those last words, her eyes drifted shut.

He really needed to make sure he didn't swear as much around her. He got under the blanket and snorted. Dora the Explorer. Couldn't the kid have parted with Spiderman?

Carys' body twitched, and he knew that she was on her way to a deep sleep. She rolled her head and some of her hair drifted onto her face. She whimpered and swiped at it. As he had done when she was awake, he brushed it back, marveling at the softness of her skin. She sighed and visibly relaxed. She melted against him, and Cullen thought he was going to have trouble going to sleep, but he forced himself to close his eyes and unwind. The last thing he was aware of was Carys cuddling closer, and a feeling of bone-deep satisfaction.

Cullen came awake, but his wrist wasn't vibrating so it wasn't his alarm. He listened intently and heard the soft sounds of Carys' breath as she snuggled closer to his chest. It had been an hour, maybe two, when he felt her arms slip around him, and it had settled them both. Now he listened even harder, then he heard what had woken him up. It was Adam.

Cullen reluctantly extricated himself from Carys' arms. He looked down at his watch. It wasn't quite midnight, but close enough for the little tyke's midnight feeding. He wanted to get to him before he went into a full roar and woke the women. The little kid struck him as someone with a fierce enough nature already to wake the whole damn desert to get what he wanted. Cullen grinned as he crept out of the back of the truck.

When he opened the front seat door, Adam was opening his mouth and sucking in air for a loud wail. Cullen was ready. He had gotten some strips of sterile gauze while he had been at the clinic, and while Carys had been eating, he had tied one of them around a tongue depressor and made it into a makeshift little pacifier that he'd wetted with water. He dunked that sucker into Adam's little mouth before he could make another cry.

"Hold on, Bubba, Uncle Cullen's going to get you

your food. Then he's going to get that stinky old diaper changed."

He prayed that the baby wasn't going to end up being inconsolable. His teammate Zed had told him some horror stories about Lulu as a newborn when he and Marcia couldn't find anything wrong with her, and she'd just cry and cry, and the only thing that would make it nominally better was if they walked her up and down the halls.

As quick as he could, he used the cigarette lighter to heat some water to mix the formula. Adam was pushing at the little pacifier, which was not going to get the job done much longer. After he mixed the formula, Cullen grabbed the baby and a clean diaper, then exited the truck with the bottle.

"Let's go take a stroll," he whispered.

He cooled a couple of drops of formula onto his finger and let the kid suck on his finger as he walked swiftly into the night. At his first screams, they were well away from the women. The bottle still needed a couple more minutes to cool.

"Do you need a serenade?" Cullen tried singing and rocking, but it didn't work. But it kind of soothed Cullen, so he continued until the formula cooled, then finally he plopped the nipple into the crying baby's mouth. Finally, there was blessed silence.

"No wonder Zed's ass was dragging when he came to the training center in the mornings," Cullen mused. He'd seen Lulu in a temper as she turned two years old, and he'd bet as a newborn she had been tremendously demanding.

When Adam was finally satisfied, Cullen got his diaper changed and then put him back down for another hour or two of sleep. He peeked in to see how Shada was doing, and her breathing was strong and regular. He smiled.

When he crawled under the blanket, he wasn't surprised when Carys sleepily asked after the mother and baby. Cullen looked at her. He wondered if she was really even awake.

"They're fine."

"Good," she slurred. In less than a minute, her breathing evened out and she was back asleep. He gathered her close and drifted off with her.

~

"Up and at 'em, Sweets." Carys' eyes popped open. It took just a moment to orient herself. She sat up in the back of the truck and saw that the truck bed was open, and Cullen was shirtless and holding Adam next to his chest as he swayed back and forth.

"Does he need to be fed?" she asked groggily.

"Nope, just did it. This was number three, right after I cleaned up number two. He sure does like to poop," Cullen grinned.

A laugh popped out of her mouth. "That's kind of what they're known for, crying, pooping and eating."

"Well, he's setting records. It's about time for us to get going."

"I need to check on Shada."

"Her saline is about empty, so I figured we would

leave a little early so you could get that done. Plus, you need to have cake for breakfast."

"Shada first." She climbed down and smoothed her finger down Adam's cheek, coming perilously close to the heat of Cullen's chest. He had kept his shirt on last night when she'd slept with him, but he was giving the baby the skin-to-skin contact she had recommended. She stifled a sigh, yearning to feel that same heat against her flesh. Embarrassed at the thought, she rushed past them to get to Shada.

By the time she switched the saline and got Shada out for yet *another* potty break and belted back up, Cullen had everything ready for them to head out. He handed her the cake and Adam.

"It's going to be bumpy, but soon we'll be on a highway," he flashed her a grin.

"Have you called your team?"

"It's going to take us forty-five minutes to an hour to get to the highway. They are cooking something up. They said to make our way there, and they'd have something for us by the time we got there."

Carys' stomach clenched. "Will they?"

"Absolutely. If they said they'll have something, they'll have something."

She searched Cullen's features. He really didn't look stressed out.

"You're really not worried?"

"Nope. They sounded confident. They have something in mind. We're going to be golden."

14

*H*e pulled onto the highway. Carys held his satellite phone so tightly that her knuckles were white, yet somehow her other hand was gently stroking Adam's head as he slept in the sling against her chest. Kane had called eighteen minutes ago to say they would have an update soon, but that Cullen and Carys should get onto the highway as planned.

The sun was just beginning to crest on the horizon. Why the hell were there so many cars on the highway? This highway was normally as empty as Route 66 in August. It should be dead. At least all the cars were headed south, away from Khartoum.

"It has to be bad in the city if this many people are fleeing," Carys said quietly. She gasped. Cullen hated it, he had hoped she wouldn't notice the small incident up ahead. Apparently, that was too much to ask for.

"What's going on?"

"RSF," he said succinctly.

"Yes, but what are they doing to those people? It looks like a family. I see children."

Carys let out a muffled shriek as she watched one of the civilian men hit in the head by the butt of a rifle. Cullen just drove faster past the spectacle.

"What could he have possibly done to deserve that?"

"Probably nothing," Cullen said. His hands were getting sweaty on the steering wheel. He glanced down at the phone in Carys' hand, willing it to ring.

They had approximately eighty kilometers to cover before they made it to the city barricade. He saw an armored combat vehicle approaching with two men manning the gun at the top. It barreled down the highway, pushing cars out of its way. Cullen swerved into the gravel on the side of the road to avoid them. Shada groaned with pain and Adam let out a sharp cry as he was jerked around.

Cullen righted the truck and continued to drive north, shutting out the sounds of Shada and Adam, and Carys' attempts to soothe them both. He needed to stay focused, not just on his driving but on any more Rapid Support Forces that might be coming their way.

The phone rang and Carys shot her hand out toward him. He grabbed it.

"Yeah? Whatcha got?"

"It's Kane. I've got a lock on you. I'm coming toward you. I'm halfway between you and Khartoum. Raiden's behind me. We're going to convoy you in."

Cullen didn't spend his time asking stupid questions like how'd they make it out of city past the barriers. "What are you driving?" Cullen asked so that he would know what to be on the lookout for.

"I'm driving the VW Kumelwagen. It's the color of mud."

"You mean *The Thing*?" Cullen couldn't help the sharp laugh that popped out of his mouth. It felt good, he needed the relief.

He saw Carys giving him the side-eye.

"Yep I think Rommel rode in it during World War II," Kane chuckled. "Raiden's stuck driving a Toyota four-runner. He lost the coin toss."

"What color is Raiden's truck?"

"It's baby blue. You said you were in a puke yellow Unimog, right? We'll see you since I'm tracking you. We'll be pulled over on your side of the road before you get past us. As soon as we see you coming in our rear-view mirrors, I'll pull out in front of you."

"What's the situation in Khartoum?"

"It's a shitstorm, but yours is a goatfuck, so you and Carys are the priority," Kane said succinctly.

"Great."

"Exactly. We should have taken the mission in Chad. Keep your head down, Lyons. Don't worry, we've got this."

The line went dead. He handed the phone back to Carys without taking his eyes away from the highway.

"What is a goatfuck?" she asked. "For that matter, what's a shitstorm?"

Cullen laughed without any humor. Then he realized she'd just sworn. "Put down the phone and give me your hand," he said as he reached out. When he felt her warm palm hit his, he twined their fingers together.

"I'm scared," she admitted quietly.

"Ahhh, Baby. I know. But the good news is that we have the two best men I know, coming to cover our ass."

"Friends of mine have died, and Shada's two little girls are in the middle of the poop-storm, I'm not seeing an upside." Carys' voice wobbled.

He snorted out a laugh. "You said poop-storm. For someone who's scared, you have quite the sense of humor."

"I guess that's a good thing, right?" she asked.

"Absolutely, Carys, it is. You amaze me." Reluctantly, he untangled their fingers, but he brought her hand over to his leg and placed it on top of his thigh. "I need to use both hands to drive."

"I understand," she whispered. They continued on in silence. She was even quiet when they passed a bus pulled over with all its passengers kneeling at the side of the road, their hands clasped behind their heads as four armed men stood behind them.

As the minutes passed by, Cullen started to slow down. He knew the petrol station was coming up. He'd been counting on it. Even from the highway, he could see at least four RSF Jeeps parked alongside the pumps. Armed RSF troops patrolled around the perimeter.

This had now escalated past a goatfuck. Maybe an albino-yak-fuck? What in the hell had happened in just three days?

"Carys, give me the phone."

She handed it to him.

"What's going on?" Kane asked.

"The petrol station I was planning to stop at is overrun by rebels. I'm going to run out of fuel in thirty kilometers or less. I need a contingency plan. Any ideas?"

Cullen could almost hear Kane's mind grinding through options. Apparently, he wasn't coming up with any, because he wasn't talking.

"I'll call you back," Kane finally said. "Don't worry."

The line went dead.

Up on the left side of the highway a huge pillar of smoke was coming up. Carys' nails dug into his thigh as she saw it too.

"Was that Kane again?" she asked.

He nodded.

"He sure tells you not to worry a lot, is that normal?"

Cullen's lip twitched upwards. The phone rang again. Before Cullen had a chance to answer it, all hell broke loose.

Another armored combat vehicle came down the middle of the highway, causing vehicles on both sides to swerve to the shoulder—what there was of one. Carys answered the phone. Cullen had no idea what she was saying, all his concentration was on the road.

Cullen watched as a car going south was hit and careened into northbound traffic up ahead. There were no guardrails, no nothing on their side of the road only gravel that fell off into a gulley. One, then two cars plowed into one another, the third skidded sideways and the fourth ended up going into the southbound traffic as the armored vehicle bared down toward Cullen's Unimog.

He knew that he didn't have anyone crawling up his ass because no one was anxious to go into Khartoum, so he hit the brakes. But it still wasn't good enough as one of the cars in front of him spun around and skidded toward him.

He wrenched the steering wheel and headed to the shoulder, bouncing over the gravel, and he drove the Unimog damn near at a ninety-degree angle along the side of the gulley, maneuvering around one car that was beginning to smolder. At last he was past the wreckage, but the truck's wheels skidded in the gulley gravel. For a moment, Cullen didn't think they would gain enough traction to make it back up the hill, but they caught, and they were back up onto the highway.

Adam was wailing.

Shada was screaming.

He turned to look at Carys, worried that she and the baby might have been injured. She was bent over in the seat, her arms tightly wrapped around the baby. In one trembling hand she still held onto the phone.

He pulled over to the side of the road. He took a deep breath.

"Honey, are you okay?"

She looked up and swallowed, her green eyes huge in her pale face. "I'm fine." She pressed the phone at him, then tugged free of her seatbelt as she quickly scanned the screaming baby.

"Is he good?"

She just nodded.

"Give him to me." Shada's screams had turned into moans. "Check on Shada."

She unwrapped Adam from his sling, and carefully handed the squalling child to Cullen. He looked around them. It was cramped as hell in the truck, but there was no way he was going to risk going outside on the highway or go into the bed of the truck with the newborn—he wouldn't put Adam into that kind of risky situation.

Carys was opening her door. He dropped the phone and grabbed her arm. "No."

"What? I need to get back there."

"Crawl over the seat. I don't want you outside this truck, it's too dangerous on the highway right now."

She scowled but nodded. Then she scooped up the phone that he'd ignored and handed it to him as she somehow managed to twist and wiggle her way over the front seat.

He heard Shada's groan of pain as Carys landed.

Fuck.

But it couldn't be helped.

"Cullen! Answer me." It was Raiden's voice on the phone. He did not sound happy.

"I'm here," Cullen answered above Adam's cries.

"Explain to me what is going on, it'll make it easier for me to help you."

You had to hand it to Sato, he knew how to sound calm in any situation. Cullen explained about the wreck and that they were on the side of the road.

"Perfect. It will make it that much easier to stop and fill you with fuel."

"So, you want me to stay here?" He did not like this plan. Not at all. "How long will it take you to get here?"

"Twenty minutes. I'm going to be the one to stop. I might have lost the coin toss, but my vehicle doesn't stick out like Kane's."

"Get here faster, Raiden, because if the RSF stops here at the wreckage site, they're going to see Carys' ass up in the air in the backseat working on Shada, and me in the front seat with Adam. I don't care if I'm in a thobe or not, it's going to be suspicious as hell."

"I promise you, I will be there as fast as humanly possible."

"Be faster than a human."

"Roger that."

~

Carys wanted to scream.

She wanted to cry.

The blanket that covered Shada was bloody, that meant that the bandage and the sheet beneath the blanket had to be soaked in blood. The only blessing was that Shada had passed out when she landed on her legs.

Carys unbuckled her and unwrapped her from the bedding as fast as she could. When she took off the bandage, she could see that blood was still pumping out of the incision. The surgical site had dehisced, opened up, probably due to infection and made worse by the driving, and now the woman was in danger of wound evisceration—an organ could actually protrude through the wound. *And if the blood's coming from a tear in her abdominal aorta...*

Carys backed up on her hands and knees, and opened the back passenger door, praying that Cullen's tie down of the medical kit had held up during their near-miss.

"Carys," Cullen roared when he heard the truck door being opened. She ignored him and got out. She didn't bother to respond. What was the point, she was going to do what needed to be done, with or without his permission.

She saw two people standing next to their vehicle, and one person kneeling next to someone lying on the ground near a car that was on fire. She ignored it all. She had to get back to Shada with her kit, or she would die for sure.

"Thank God," she breathed when she saw that the kit was still in place. She untethered it, pulled it out of the truck bed and sprinted back to the door she'd left open.

"Don't you ever fucking do that again," Cullen yelled over Adam's crying.

There wasn't time for a pissing match, so she ignored him. Carys swung the med kit up onto the little available space in the already crowded backseat. She knew what she needed, it was a matter of getting to it in time.

The other back seat door slammed open. Carys looked up and saw a steely eyed Cullen standing there. "Put me to work, Doc. Adam's fine where he is."

"Apply pressure to the wound. I think her

abdominal aorta is leaking, tissues probably weakened by infection." She tossed over some gauze as she dug down to the bottom of the kit. Dr. Nazer had helped to pack the kit, but she had put in the QuikClot packets. Her darn bloody hands were so slippery she was having trouble feeling for things.

She gasped with relief as she pulled out the two packages. She tore the first one open with her teeth and looked up.

"Ready?" she asked Cullen. He nodded.

He lifted his hands and removed the gauze from the bloody wound, and she stuffed it with the combat gauze, getting right in there next to the aorta, just in case. She continued to apply it until she could see that the hemostatic agents in the QuikClot were doing their job and stopping the bleeding. It wasn't a cure-all, but, God willing, it would last long enough to get her to the hospital in Khartoum.

She looked up and saw that Cullen's white robes were now covered in blood, so was her light brown robes, but at least it blended in a little better.

"Take off your thobe. If we're pulled over, we're going to be in worse trouble than if you're in your uniform. Can you get the tight pants and soccer jersey?"

He nodded and closed his door.

Carys efficiently bundled up Shada. Once again, the mother was out cold. She took her blood pressure which was terribly low. She switched out the bag of saline, which was all she could do at this point, and once again buckled her into the car.

She shimmied out of the backseat, dragging her medical kit with her. She started to turn to see what was happening with the others along the side of the road. She couldn't resist, if she could help, she was going to help.

"Ah. Ah. Ah." A mammoth chest covered in red blocked her view. "Get into the car, Carys."

"But—" she started to protest.

Cullen tipped her chin up until she stared into his steely blue eyes. "Get in the car. It's not safe out here. Adam and Shada need you."

She closed her eyes. Cullen was right. She needed to prioritize. But maybe if she—?

He snagged the kit out of her hands, pulled open the passenger seat door. "Pick up Adam, he's scared as hell. You can't leave him like that, can you?"

She saw the baby where he was squalling, his arms waving in his makeshift bed on the floor of the truck. All thoughts of other people along side of the road left her for the moment.

"Get your butt inside," he commanded as she picked up the baby.

He shut the door behind her after she sat down. She rocked Adam, trying to get him to settle, waiting for Cullen to get into the driver's seat. It took minutes for her to realize that he wasn't coming back. Where was he?

She turned around in her seat and saw him crouched over the man who was passed out beside the road. Now she was ready to open her truck door, his eyes shot up to look at her. Even from forty yards away, she could see his command. She was to stay where she was. She peeked over the seat to look at Shada and held on tighter to the screaming baby who needed to be fed.

"Lyons!" a voice roared.

That was when she noticed the blue Toyota truck and Raiden Sato.

15

*C*ullen walked away from the dead man. He wanted to slam the medical kit into the back of the truck for all the good it had done. He'd heard Raiden, but he needed just thirty seconds to get his head on straight before the next crisis, so he took it by tying down the bag into the truck bed.

He peered into the back seat where Shada was, the cloth that had been covering the back window was long gone. He could see that even with her naturally dark skin tone, she looked pallid and wan. He still wanted to get his hands on the man who had beat her up. The thought of torturing that bastard put a grim smile on his face. He turned to look at Raiden.

The man already had the nozzle of the jerry can shoved into the filler neck and was transferring fuel into the truck. "What's going on at the city? Why the hell is Carys' name on a hit list? Who was killed? Basically, what in the hell went so damned FUBAR in

Khartoum?" Cullen demanded low enough so Carys couldn't hear.

Raiden's face went blank. Stone cold solid. Cullen's stomach clenched.

It was going to be bad.

So bad.

"It started out fine. It always starts out with good intentions, doesn't it?" Raiden's voice was a trace of its normal level, but his words' impact was easily heard over the highway traffic. "The people had had enough of the brutality of the Rapid Support Forces. The killings and rapes had started, but when two people were doused with gasoline and..."

Raiden didn't need to finish the sentence. The same things had occurred last summer. The same violence had precipitated Hamdok coming into power.

"The people took to the streets. First it was the students, in less than twenty-four hours it escalated to tens of thousands. They were out for blood. They wanted to take down everybody in authority. They set the first government building on fire thirty hours ago. Soon, not just the RSF were targeted, but anyone in uniform. Countries all over the world have sent in their special forces to get their people the hell out of here. Captain Hale came in with the Midnight Delta crew to help us get the rest of the Americans out."

"Why? I thought we had it covered with the Marines coming in on the two Ospreys. Wasn't it just two days ago or a day and a half?" Cullen ran his hand over his head. He was confused at the timeline, just too little sleep.

"Anyway, Kane told me that it was less than two hundred Americans left to be evacuated maybe a day and a half ago, so shouldn't they all be gone? Why aren't we done?"

"There's a problem with that. The bomb that went off at the embassy hit their computer system. They gave us the wrong initial numbers. We've since got updated numbers from the back-up server in the US. So as of an hour ago, we have over three hundred Americans to evacuate, that's another reason why Captain Hale is here."

"FUBAR," Cullen bit out.

"You do have a way with words," Raiden said.

"You still haven't answered my other questions."

"Now isn't the time. I'll tell you when we get to the hospital in the city."

Cullen nodded. "Where's Kane? I thought we were convoying."

"I'm taking the lead. Kane's two klicks up the road, he's going to come in on your tail."

Cullen nodded, they gripped hands and stared at one another for a moment. Everything was conveyed without words.

"Still think I should lead, your Toyota is a loser." Cullen scoffed.

"But I'm the better driver," Raiden smiled before he hot-footed back to his truck.

Why do people, men in particular, think that they can say things and not be heard?

Why?

She waited to ask until after Cullen got buckled in and the truck started up. She wanted to make sure they could ease up along the shoulder and were able to safely follow Raiden.

"What is—"

"Fouled Up Beyond All Recognition," Cullen answered her question before she had a chance to ask it.

"How did you—?"

"I didn't leave the window rolled down even a little bit. Now it is. You were listening." He glanced over at her and gave her a wide grin. "I totally would have done the same thing."

"You guys use a different word than 'fouled' don't you?"

"Yes, ma'am."

Carys sat back in the seat and continued to feed Adam his warmed-up bottle. She went over everything they'd said. After her time in Greece, she had taught herself to become hard in the face of tragedy, it was the only way to survive. But she hated the person she had become. That was the reason she had left DWB. The eight months she'd been in the States had helped get her right in the head. But here she was again—dull, lifeless, uncaring.

"Carys, it's going to be okay."

"I know."

Cullen's warm hand snuck under her braid to clasp around the back of her neck. She jolted, then settled into his gentle caress. "Talk to me, Honey."

"About what? FUBAR?" Her voice sounded funny.

"Ah, Carys, you're crying. Do you mean to be giving Adam his first shower?"

Carys touched her cheek. Her finger was trembling too.

"I'm not supposed to be crying. I'm made of stone. I don't care about things."

Cullen snorted as his thumb stroked up the middle line of her neck, hitting the base of her scalp. "Relax your head. Just let it tilt down."

"You need both hands on the wheel." Her voice was slurring, his hand felt like molten gold, sinking into every physical and emotional hurt.

"Raiden and Kane are protecting us. Let me help you." Distantly she saw Adam's eyes drift shut. She set the bottle down next to her and soothed circles over his tummy as she soaked in Cullen's touch.

"Talk to me, Carys."

She didn't respond.

He waited and continued to press in, stroking and swirling his fingers in just a way that melted her muscles and dissolved her hurt. How could one man's touch make her feel so treasured?

"It's just too much," she finally answered. "But I promise I'll be fine when we get to Khartoum. I won't let you down."

"There is no way in hell you could ever let me down, Carys." Cullen's thumb brushed the top of her spine. When a tendril of hair worked its way loose from her braid, his fingers were immediately there to tuck it back into her hair's twist. Adam began to get fussy.

"I need to burp him."

"We're circling back to this when we have time," Cullen warned. "I don't want you hurting."

She put the baby on her shoulder and gently patted his back. She took a look over at Cullen, his attention was on the road. She looked up and saw another group of people pulled over, soldiers standing over them with guns.

Would it never end?

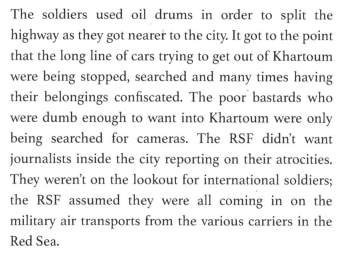

The soldiers used oil drums in order to split the highway as they got nearer to the city. It got to the point that the long line of cars trying to get out of Khartoum were being stopped, searched and many times having their belongings confiscated. The poor bastards who were dumb enough to want into Khartoum were only being searched for cameras. The RSF didn't want journalists inside the city reporting on their atrocities. They weren't on the lookout for international soldiers; the RSF assumed they were all coming in on the military air transports from the various carriers in the Red Sea.

Unfortunately, the angry older man who was checking their car, did have some extra questions for Cullen and Carys, especially when Carys could not produce identification. Ever since Cullen found out about Carys being on a watch list, he'd had her I.D. taped to the bottom of one of the crates supporting Shada's mattress.

"Who is this woman and baby to you? Why are the two of you taking her to the hospital? Why not a Sudanese driver and nurse from Wad Madani?"

Carys jumped in before Cullen even had a chance to spin his normal bullshit.

"This young woman's father used to work at the American Embassy. He left his job six months ago, but when he heard that my husband and I were travelling from Wad Madani to Khartoum he insisted that we bring her. He knew that I was a nurse and my husband would be a good escort because he once was a law enforcement officer in America."

His head swiveled to look at Cullen. "She is your wife?"

"Yes," Cullen affirmed.

"Let me talk to my supervisor."

As soon as he walked away, Cullen called Kane. He wished he had his normal mic and receiver system, but they weren't on a normal mission, so there had been no point. He kept his phone out of sight on his lap.

"Kane, we've got a problem, he's going to talk to his supervisor, I need a diversion."

"You got it," Kane said.

Even though Kane had already been waved through, he had only gone a hundred meters beyond the checkpoint. Cullen grinned as he saw him turn the *Thing* around and then do a three-hundred and sixty degree turn into on-coming traffic. He pulled his gun out and shot into the air.

"Well, that's sure a diversion," Carys deadpanned.

They watched as four of the current men manning

their checkpoints jumped into Jeeps to follow Kane. Cullen knew that those men would be toast.

The man who had been questioning them came back and threw Cullen's fake I.D. back through the window. "Just go," he said in disgust. When it took Cullen a moment to start the vehicle, he hit the roof of the truck angrily. "I said go!"

Adam started to cry and Cullen put the truck in gear and sighed with relief as he made it onto the main street of Khartoum.

"Raiden said to take her to the same hospital where you were before. Some of our guys have it secured. I'm going to call ahead."

"Have them put one of my people on the line, I'll tell them what I need."

Cullen's gut clenched. He was pretty sure that there was bad news, really bad news regarding her team, but now wasn't the time to tell her. He placed a call to his lieutenant, Max Hogan, who didn't pick up. He went down the line until he got ahold of Nick Hale, the junior member of their team.

"Where are you, Nick?"

"I'm leaving the airport now. The lieutenant said I needed to get my ass to the Khartoum General Hospital and meet up with all y'all."

"Is it up and running?"

"It's one of the few. The Marines, and a couple of SEALs from the Midnight Delta team, have it covered. Nobody is messing with it."

Cullen looked over at Carys who was nodding that she was hearing everything. "I'm going to put Dr.

Adams on the line. She's going to tell you what she needs when she arrives. Everything needs to move slick as snot when we get there. You got that?"

"One oiled pig coming up."

Cullen slowed the truck down as he rolled down the window. He motioned for Raiden to come up beside him. When he could see his friend, he yelled over to him. "Get us past all of this mess to Khartoum General." He motioned his hand toward the mob in the street in front of him.

Raiden nodded, and pulled out in front of him. He took an immediate left down a side street. Cullen followed. Before they got to another huge cluster of protesters with signs and banners, Raiden took a right going down a one-way street the wrong way, but it worked.

Cullen continued to blindly follow his teammate.

Right.

Left.

Left.

Right.

Finally, he did a fast turn into a parking lot that Cullen didn't recognize, but he continued on, four-wheeling over the double curb that took them to the back entrance of the hospital.

Nick and two orderlies appeared like fucking magic rolling a gurney down the back ramp. Nick had a huge grin on his face like he'd just solved world hunger. "Somebody need a ride?" he called out above the screeching of the Unimog's tires. As soon as Cullen stopped the truck and put it in park, Carys handed

Cullen the baby. She was out the door and shouting orders as she opened the back passenger door.

The orderlies gently lifted the entire mattress with Shada on it, onto the gurney. Carys held the bag of saline high above her head.

"Nick! Come here." Cullen shouted. Before Nick could get to his door, Raiden was there, opening the door and taking Adam into his arms.

"Your doctor has it under control, but I know I'd want to be there, so go," Raiden nodded toward the doors that had just closed.

Cullen ran up the rampway.

16

"*S*ir, you can't go in there," the thin nurse said emphatically in Arabic.

"Yes, I can," Cullen growled. He was not going to be stopped at this point. Carys and Shada were behind those doors. He needed to make sure they were all right. That was his job, they were his mission.

A security guard and an orderly appeared behind the thin nurse. Cullen's expression turned feral. Like *they* were going to stop him.

"Lyons, stand down." Raiden called out in English. He heard Adam crying behind him.

He turned. There was Raiden. He was unruffled despite holding a baby who was trying to blow down the walls of the hospital with his screams.

"Dr. Adams is going to take good care of her patient," the nurse assured Cullen. Her voice was just loud enough to be heard above Adam's cries.

Cullen went over to Raiden, "Give Bubba to me."

He turned back to the nurse. "He needs formula, a bath, and a clean diaper. Where can I take of him?"

"I'll take care of him," she said as she held out her arms.

"That's not what I asked," Cullen said. He just barely kept his voice civil. He was tired, really hungry and worried as hell. Not just for Shada, but for Carys, she was going to be devastated if Shada didn't come out of this alive.

"Ma'am, this little boy is very important to me, we've been through a lot. I would like to take care of him myself. Is there a place where I can get him cleaned up and fed?"

She frowned. "You need to be clean before you are allowed into our nursery."

"He could go into the doctor's locker room," the orderly suggested. "They have a shower. I could find him some scrubs."

"Will you allow me to bathe him while you shower, sir? Then you can feed him?" the nurse asked.

It was the right thing to do, so Cullen nodded.

That was why Kane McNamara and two of his friends from Midnight Delta found him in the waiting room, freshly showered in white scrubs, feeding a baby.

Kane dumped a bag on the chair beside him. The smell was heavenly. Cullen grunted with laughter when he saw what it said, Chicking Fried Chicken.

"It was that or hospital food."

"Adam gets fed first," Cullen said. "Then me."

"I'll burp him," a big blond man with a Texas accent said as he walked into the waiting room.

Cullen grinned. "What do you know about burping babies, Jack?" he asked the big SEAL who was on the Midnight Delta team.

"I'm getting into practice for our daughter. She's due in two months. Beth will be impressed that I got in some practice while I was over here."

"You really have time to be burping babies?" Kane asked Jack Preston. "I knew you guys from California didn't work." Cullen handed Adam over to Jack who handled him pretty good. Not perfect, but pretty good.

"Watch your tongue—you idiots from D.C. are the ones who can never get anything done," Drake Avery said. He was the second-in-command of the Midnight Delta team.

God, that man could start a fight in a meditation studio.

"We're not from D.C., you over-sized Tennessee asshole," Kane thundered. "We're from Virginia. If I didn't like your wife so much, I'd wipe up the floor with you, right here and right now."

"Great, Drake, once again you have endeared us to another SEAL team. Burp Adam and shut up." Jack handed over Adam to the largest man in the room. "When you see him with a baby, he becomes a palatable human being."

If Cullen hadn't been so hungry, and he didn't know Drake, there was no way he would have allowed Adam to be handed over to the senseless SEAL.

"So why are you two here?" Cullen asked.

"We're here to update you guys on a couple of things."

Cullen handed over a burp towel to Drake, then ripped open the fast food bag.

"What info do you have?" Raiden asked.

"All Embassy personnel have finally made it out of the country on this last flight to Egypt. The airport is now tighter than a tick. We're cleared for incoming flights and outgoing flights, our problem is just getting people into the airport."

Cullen approved of the way that Drake swayed back and forth with Adam and lightly rubbed his back.

"How many people still need to be evac'd?" Raiden asked.

"We're down to approximately two-hundred fifty Americans. About a quarter of them we're having to go door-to-door to get."

"Is anybody else helping, or does it all come down to us?" Kane asked as he handed a chicken sandwich to Raiden and offered one up to Drake who shook his head.

"Now that all the spec ops from the other countries are here, they helped to secure the airport, so some of the Marines that came from the *USS Autry* when the Ospreys landed are helping us. All-in-all, we have twenty-three of us on this project. Captain Hale is holed up with our two lieutenants—he wants every American out of Sudan by EOD tomorrow."

The bite he had just taken turned to dust in Cullen's mouth. Until they figured out how to ensure Shada and her children were safe, he didn't think there was a chance in hell that Carys was going to leave.

Cullen woke up disoriented. Raiden crouched over him.

"Man, I've never seen you sleep so deep."

"Is Carys out of surgery?"

"A nurse came out. She said things are wrapping up. Carys should be out soon."

Cullen looked around and remembered that someone had pointed him to the relative quiet of the couch in the doctor's lounge. God, he'd needed the sleep. For that matter, so did Carys. She had to be dead on her feet.

He followed his friend out to the waiting room. Kane, Jack and Drake were gone. "Where is everybody? Where's Adam?"

"Drake went down to coordinate with the Marines. Jack and Kane are doing house-to-house sweeps for civilians to evacuate. As for Adam, you don't have to worry about him, he's asleep in the nursery with the other babies," Raiden assured him. "I put an extra security guard on the floor and one right outside the nursery while I checked in with the lieutenant."

He looked at Raiden for three extra heartbeats, trying to comprehend what his friend just told him. "Why the extra security?"

"Leila told the guy who tried to snatch her that her mom gave birth to a son. On the outside chance that her bastard of a father might want to get his hands on him, I didn't want to take any risks."

"Makes sense," Cullen nodded. He still wasn't firing

on all cylinders as he looked around the ugly beige room where they forced family to wait for news about their loved ones. He longed for some coffee, but something else occurred to him. "Where are Leila and Aamira? Jesus, what about Farida, please tell me she's all right. She is, isn't she?"

"Whoa there," Raiden said as Cullen grabbed his shoulders. "I'm not keeping them from you. The two oldest girls are at a hotel with Faizah, and Farida is actually here. They ended up having to remove her spleen."

Cullen knew that wasn't too bad, he'd had friends who did just fine without a spleen. But he could tell by Raiden's expression there was more. "Out with it," he demanded.

"They found an old fracture on one of her ribs. That bastard had had his hands on her before this."

"And the other girls? They were looked over too, right?"

"Yes," Raiden assured him. "They're fine now, but x-rays showed that they had old injuries. Besides Aamira's arm not being set properly, they found a hairline fracture on Leila's skull. These girls have been used as punching bags. Thank God we got Leila away from her father's lackey before she could be taken back to that bastard."

"As long as the girls are safe now, and Farida is on the mend, that's what matters." Cullen felt some of the weight he'd been carrying lift. But he knew there was a lot more that Raiden had to tell him.

"Tell me about Carys' team and do it quick. I want to be the one who breaks the news to her."

"I told you about the list that the RSF had with Carys' name on it, right?"

Cullen nodded.

"Well every single one of Carys' particular team were on it. Not all the DWB group that came in from the states, just the nine who were assembled by Carys."

"That doesn't make any sense," Cullen protested. He dropped down into one of the uncomfortable waiting room chairs. "Explain it to me."

"It turns out that a doctor by the name of Joyce Dandekar was instrumental in getting Carys' team invited over here. Joyce and Carys studied together in the States. She was the fiancée of one of the generals in the Transitional Military Council."

"Was? You're not going to tell me they had a bad break-up, are you?"

Raiden sat down across from him.

"No, I'm not. When that general was overthrown during one of the many coups, she was declared an enemy of the state, as was Carys' team. Joyce has been captured and killed. The only ones left alive on Carys' team are a Nurse Harris and a Dr. Phong. They've both been evacuated."

"What about the two that were missing? Any hope for them?"

"No, their bodies were found with Doctor Dandekar's."

This was going to kill Carys when she found out.

"How long did the nurse say until the surgery wraps up?" Cullen asked.

"Twenty to thirty minutes," Raiden answered.

Cullen really looked at his friend, and saw he was showing signs of wear and tear too. "Let's go grab a cup of coffee, and you can fill me in on some good news. There is good news, right?"

"I do have a couple of pieces of good news," Raiden agreed. They both pushed up from their seats at the same time. Raiden looked down at his watch, "We maybe have ten minutes. Leila gave me a piece of paper with that mythical uncle in Egypt that Shada had told us about, and I gave it to Kane. Turns out he's real."

"No way," Cullen was stunned. That kind of shit never happened. "Did Kane contact him, is he willing to help?"

"He is. He doesn't have much, but he has a shop, and Shada and her little family could live in the apartment above the store. He wants to come and meet them after things settle down."

Cullen thought his heart might beat out of his chest. *Now that's the way a book should end, with a happily ever after. They never did, but that's the way they should.*

When they got to the front of the line, the clerk asked them if they would like their coffee in to-go cups or mugs. They chose cups and headed back upstairs. Raiden looked at his watch. "So, you're sure Leila doesn't have any lasting effects from the almost-kidnapping?" Cullen asked.

"Yeah, sure, like I've had time to check on that." It

was one of the few times Raiden Sato sounded sarcastic and Cullen laughed.

"I guess I've gotten into babysitting mode, instead of SEAL mode. I'll talk to Faizah. Raiden, this has been a weird mission. I'm now into Daddy-duty."

"I don't know, Lyons, I think it did more than that. I saw how you were looking at the good doctor. You're reminding me of Kane with A.J. when we had the mission in Oman."

"Ah, he didn't know he was in it for the long haul right from the get-go, the dumb son-of-a-bitch. It was funnier than hell to see the writing on the wall and have him so oblivious," Cullen said over his shoulder as he looked toward the door leading to the operating rooms.

"What do you mean?" Raiden asked. "He knew he wanted A.J. from day one."

"Yeah, but he didn't realize that she was the one for him. The one he was going to make a life with."

Cullen tossed his empty cup in the trash and crossed his arms, willing the door to open.

Raiden grasped his shoulder to turn him around. "Are you telling me that you're in love with Carys?"

"Yep. Not only that, I'm going to marry that woman."

Raiden just stared at him and gave a half-laugh. "Are you kidding?"

"Nope, I'm serious as a heart attack." Cullen replied.

"I don't understand you at all. That makes no sense."

"Sure it does," Cullen laughed. "It's a tradition passed down throughout the men in my family."

Raiden shook his head in disbelief. But then again, Cullen knew a little bit about his friend's past, and he could see why he wouldn't believe in finding an everlasting love in three days. Now he just had to convince Carys. He rubbed his jaw. How in the hell was he going to do that?

~

She was higher than a kite, even though she was shaky as heck. Shada had made it through surgery and the prognosis was looking good. She didn't want to jinx anything, but Carys was pretty darn sure the young mother was going to pull through and thrive. She would be there for her children! She would see her grandchildren, just as Carys had promised.

She pulled off her gown, gloves and face mask, then leaned against the scrub sink. The adrenaline that had been keeping her going for the last few hours had left her. She felt like she was going to throw up. But she would do it smiling.

"Doctor?"

"Hmmm?"

Warm hands were on her shoulders, they guided her past the sink and she soon found herself sitting in a chair with a glass of juice in her hand. Carys sipped it gratefully. She just needed a minute to get herself together, then she could go out and tell the happy news.

She couldn't wait to inform Cullen, he would be so relieved. He cared as much as she did.

She had friends who were soldiers, but she didn't think she had ever met one with a bigger heart.

A hand took the juice from her just before it spilled.

What?

"You were falling asleep, Doctor."

Carys pushed up from the chair she was sitting in. "Can you direct me to the waiting room? I think there are some people who want to know how my patient did during her surgery."

"Yes, Doctor. Follow me," the middle-aged nurse beckoned.

As the woman went to the door to push it open, there was a loud shout. It was in English. The nurse looked at Carys in confusion.

"Get to the nursery," a man yelled.

"It's too late, we need to get to the lobby," another man's voice shouted.

Was that Raiden?

~

Cullen's pounding footsteps echoed as he raced down the hospital stairs. Only four flights but he'd make it in under a minute. Raiden was one floor above him.

Adam.

It had to be his dad.

He slammed the door to the lobby open. It took a half-second to orient himself.

Left. His boot skidded and he realized someone had

just mopped. His shoulder slammed into a wall as he pinballed to one side trying to stay upright.

Fuck! Fuck!

What was this dumbass thinking? There were Marines posted outside the hospital.

Cullen had his gun out as he turned the corner into the lobby that still had plywood covering many of the windows. He squinted to adjust his vision, then he stopped short.

What the hell?

There was a crowd. Students with signs and banners, and Sudanese civilians were spilling into the lobby and the Marines were trying to stop them, but the people were ignoring them. Cullen would bet money it was a coordinated smokescreen. How Shada's husband had managed to do that, he had no idea, but he had.

Raiden was beside him. "I've got intel from a nurse. Three men demanded to know which child was Shada's baby and she wouldn't tell. They knocked her around pretty good and killed the two security guards. Slit their throats. That's why we didn't hear anything. Another nurse finally told them which baby was Adam."

"Rapid Support Forces?"

"She didn't know. She said they weren't wearing any kind of uniform."

Cullen scanned the crowd. There were just too many people. The three men could have split up. For all they knew, Adam could have been passed off to one of the women in the crowd.

He looked around, trying to come up with some

sort of way to find Bubba. Like a beacon of light, he saw his solution on the wall. Then he looked up—sure as shit, there were sprinkler heads on the ceiling. He ran to the wall.

"Grab the Marines and cover the hospital entrance," he yelled to Raiden as he ran to the fire alarm.

"Fire," he yelled out in Arabic at the top of his lungs, as he pulled the fire alarm lever.

He turned and saw the Marines and Raiden holding their weapons, stopping anyone from leaving the lobby through the front entrance. Everyone got soaked as they screamed in horror, begging to be let out. Cullen knew that he was causing havoc in the rest of the hospital, but he didn't care. His sole focus was on finding Adam.

Like rats on a sinking ship, he saw two drenched men in thobes coming toward him trying to exit the back way since they knew their way around the hospital.

"Cullen," someone yelled from down the back hall behind him. Was that Drake?

He let the first man whose arms were empty go right by, figuring his fellow SEAL would take care of him. Meanwhile, the man holding the baby—well, he wasn't going anywhere.

When the man saw Cullen, he straightened up, not caring that Adam was soaked, water streaming into his mouth.

"Let me by," he commanded. It was clear he was used to being in command.

"No way. Give me the child," Cullen said as water dripped down his face and he held out one arm, his gun in the other. The man's eyes squinted—they both knew that Cullen wasn't going to use it; he wouldn't risk Adam being hurt.

"He is my son, he stays with me."

Cullen lifted the gun higher and the man smiled. "Try it. I still have my man watching you. You will soon die."

A lie. Cullen would already be dead if that were true.

"You're a war criminal who is trying to kidnap a baby from his mother, now give me Adam." Cullen stepped forward, gripping his gun tighter.

"What kind of name is Adam?" the man's lip curled in disgust. "He will be named after my father. Nobody will deny me my son, certainly not some American thug."

The sprinklers had stopped, but why was wasn't Adam crying? Water wasn't running into his mouth anymore. Cullen saw Raiden at the edge of the crowd of students.

Cullen heard a high-pitched scream, and Drake's yell, then a shot fired from the hallway behind him.

Adam finally gave a weak cry, but not because of the noise, it was because the stupid bastard was suddenly squeezing him too tight. Goddammit, the man might end up killing his own child!

"You're hurting him," Cullen ground out as he pointed his gun at the man's head.

The man glared and pulled Adam tighter to his body. "You'll never shoot me." In a flash, he changed his grip on Adam, gripping the baby by his legs, causing him to dangle upside down in front of him as a shield. "Now I will walk away from here. If you try to shoot me, the boy falls and dies."

Raiden was directly behind him, waiting for the word from Cullen.

Cullen took two steps toward the monster who fathered four beautiful children.

"Now!" he shouted.

Raiden wasted no time. With his gun pointed upwards at the base of the man's skull, he literally shot his head off as Cullen caught Adam before he had a chance to hit the floor. They were both covered in blood, and Raiden grabbed the bastard's body so he didn't fall on them.

Adam was screaming. Cullen thought he might blow apart at the seams.

He blocked out the shouts of the crowd and the questions that swirled in his head. Instead, he cradled the child in his arms, wishing he could make him happy, but gratified he was alive to scream.

The only thing that would make this moment perfect would be to share it with Carys.

17

*S*he watched as the tiny family gathered around in Shada's curtained off recovery area. Leila and Aamira sat on chairs next to their mother's bed, both of them kicking their little legs as they ate chocolate that Cullen had procured for them. Shada's Great-Uncle Pashat from Egypt, held Farida, and Shada had Adam cuddled up beside her. It was darn near the first time Carys had seen that baby out of Cullen's arms in the last twenty-four hours.

She looked over at Cullen. His expression was hard to read. Funny, since she had thought that he would be satisfied, maybe even happy, over this turn of events. He looked up and caught her eye. Had he felt her looking at him? He gave her a slow smile. She felt her insides heating up. He moved away from the curtain that separated Shada's bed from the others in the ward and came over to her and slid his arm around her waist. It felt right. She wasn't dressed as a doctor—today she was in her travel clothes since she was going to be flying home.

"Doctor Adams," Shada's voice was hoarse. "Will we ever see you again?"

She didn't know how to answer. She hadn't been expecting the question, and she should have. She was definitely out of practice.

"Shada, Doctor Adams is going to start practicing medicine in America. It is possible she might not return to Africa. It is both our hopes that you will send us letters when you settle in Egypt. I will provide you with my information so that you can reach her."

"And you, sir. We want to write to you too," Shada smiled shyly. "You saved my son." Her voice broke.

"He gave us candy, Mama." Leila chimed in. "I will draw him pictures of our new home. Can you send us candy when we live with our Uncle?"

The old man beamed at Leila. "I will have much good food for you to eat, my girl."

"I can send you treats from America," Cullen smiled. "If everyone approves."

How come Carys had a feeling Cullen sent more than a few care packages around the world? This man was not who she had originally thought he was. He was so much more.

Carys bit her lip when she thought again about how special he was, and what he really deserved out of life.

Aamira got down off her chair and came up to Carys. "Are you going to stay until my Mama is all better?"

Once again, Carys found herself at a loss for words.

Cullen crouched down so he could talk eye-to-eye to the pretty little girl. "Honey, your Mama is going to be out of here in no time. Doctor Adams did a wonderful job making sure of that. Now she has to go home." He winked at the girl and she giggled.

Carys appreciated him talking for her. Normally that kind of thing was not the case, but she was still reeling from the deaths of all her associates. Then there was the fact that her good friend Joyce had been killed while under custody of the Rapid Support Forces. All of it just made her want to leave Khartoum as soon as possible. It was all too much.

Shada held out her hand. "Doctor?"

Carys walked over and took the woman's hand. "Yes?"

"I will always remember you. I will tell my son many stories of you. Thank you for saving both of us. *I wish that you will always walk under a thousand stars and know the kiss of the sun for your kindness is unequaled in all the universe.*"

Carys felt sandpaper scrape the backs of her eyes. "You astound me, Shada," she gulped. "Hold your children close. I hope that I *do* see you again one day." She squeezed the young mother's hand, then waved to the girls, and let Cullen lead her out of the hospital ward.

∾

Cullen got to the airport in time to see her in the big holding area with the other evacuees. His last swing through the city looking for other Americans to evacuate had cost him valuable time to get to her.

She had her backpack hanging from one shoulder. She'd arrived with more, but in the mass confusion of the uprising, she'd lost her things. As she said to him, a hell of a lot more than things had been lost. Cullen sighed, remembering she'd said *heck*.

This take-no-prisoners woman looked lost as she stood with other evacuees at the Khartoum airport. He wanted to tell her not to go, to stay with him. But hell, he was here for probably another week on clean-up duty, then he was on his way home. How could she stay? She couldn't. All civilians were supposed to leave as soon as they were located.

Hell, he *wanted* her out of the country where it was safe. But *damn*, he wanted her beside him.

"Carys?" His voice was a whisper, but she heard him.

She looked up at him, her green eyes bewildered. She'd been like that since yesterday. Shellshocked.

Goddammit, she needed him. If not him, somebody.

"Honey, where are you going when you get home?" He asked her as she tried to get close to the barrier that separated them.

"I left my things in storage in Eugene, Oregon."

"You're not going to be there all by yourself, are you?"

She must have caught onto the worry in his voice, because she hitched her backpack higher up on her shoulder and straightened her spine.

"Cullen, I'm going to be fine. I'm a big girl. I'm going to go to Eugene and get my things. I know the things I put into place before I left probably aren't there. Even if they were, I need time again before I can move forward. But you don't need to worry, I'm fine."

"You need to stay with someone. Maybe Peter?"

"No, I don't." She gave a bright fake smile.

"Yes, you do. You need to be with friends."

He didn't say she needed to be with him. But dammit, she did.

"Yeah, sure, that sounds good, I'll call him."

She was lying.

The crowd started to move.

"You have all my contact information. I need a call as soon as you land."

"Absolutely, Cullen. I'll call you. But I'm not like Shada and her family, you don't need to worry about me. I don't want to be one more burden to you."

He would have pulled her into a hug, but the barriers kept them apart.

"Dammit, Carys, that's not what this is. I *want* to see you when I get back to the states, I *need* to see you."

She shook her head, denying what he was saying. She didn't believe him.

Then the crowd swallowed her up.

Dammit!

~

A month, it had taken him an entire damn month. Cullen was so pissed as he walked up the path of two-story Craftsman style house with rhododendron and azalea bushes flourishing in the front yard. There was a trike with pink tassels coming out of the handlebars in the front yard, so there was at least one kid that Kane hadn't told him about. How'd he miss that? He'd told Cullen all about Sarah Kyle who was Carys' best friend and was now married to David Sloane. The couple had been with Carys all those years ago when she had been assaulted in Santa Flores, and Kane had tracked Carys down to their house here in Washington state.

He knocked on the front door. A pretty blonde answered. She looked him up and down and smiled.

"Honey, who is it?" A tall, lean man asked as he came up behind her.

Before Cullen could introduce himself, she answered.

"If I had to guess, this is Cullen Lyons. Am I right?" she asked with a twinkle in her eye.

Cullen frowned. All of his Irish charm bullshit had flown out the window three weeks ago when Carys texted him that she wasn't ready to face him, and that she would call him when she was ready. For eighteen days after that, there had been radio silence, then when she finally called, she said she would let him know where and when they could meet in a week.

Fuck that noise.

The man grinned. "I'm going to be barbequing tonight. Want to join us?"

"Is Carys here?"

"She's out in the backyard playing with Tonya, our

daughter. She'll be eating dinner with us. Now do you want to say yes?" the blonde asked temptingly.

"Honey, have you introduced yourself?" The man who had to be Captain David Sloane asked.

She laughed. It was a pretty laugh. "Why don't you come in, have some lemonade or sweet tea."

"Or a beer," David offered. "I'm Captain David Sloane, United States Army. You're Chief Petty Officer Cullen Lyons with the United States Navy," David said as he held out his hand.

"How do you know?"

"Same way you know about me. We've checked one another out. I figure Kane McNamara finally tracked us down and that's why you're here."

"I forgot you're Military Police," Cullen chuckled as he took the proffered beer and sat down at the kitchen stool. He scanned the backyard through the sliding glass door, but the backyard was too big, he couldn't see Carys or their daughter.

"I'm Sarah Sloane. But apparently you know that as well," Sarah smiled as she pulled out a tray of vegetables and plopped those down in front of him.

"I'm surprised you managed to stay away as long as you did," David said as he leaned on his elbows on the kitchen island across from Cullen. "I've been telling Carys to expect you at our door for the last two weeks."

"She said something about next week, but it was time to take the yak by the horns. I also wanted to do it where she had friends backing her up, in case it all goes South."

He wanted to ask them if it was going to go South.

He didn't think it would. He prayed it wouldn't. David had given him a beer. Sarah had let him into the house. Those were good signs, right? But maybe this was just because they were feeling sorry for him.

Cullen saw the diminutive girl in pink jeans running from the side of the house to the door. He then caught sight of Carys chasing slowly behind her. She was smiling. A real smile.

"Can I have some juice?" a little voice piped up as the sliding glass door opened.

"Tonya beat me again..." Carys' voice trailed off as she saw Cullen.

This was it, the big reveal.

~

Carys stopped short, she couldn't breathe.

He was here. Cullen was actually here.

She wanted to soak Cullen in through her skin. Just seeing him made her heart beat faster.

Heck, who am I kidding? Seeing him here just made my heart finally start beating again!

He looked so different in his jeans and black Henley. The man she had been dreaming about for over a month looked more laid back, more approachable, which made him so much scarier.

Africa had been one of the top three worst experiences of her entire life. But because of Cullen, she remembered parts of it with absolute joy.

How was that even possible?

Cullen set down the beer he had been holding, got off the kitchen stool and prowled over to her.

"Mom, who's he?" she heard Tonya ask.

"Carys, can we go outside?" His low voice vibrated through her body.

She looked up into those tempting blue eyes and nodded, because she didn't have enough air to speak. He lightly touched her lower back as he opened the sliding glass door and guided her outside. His hand felt like it offered her protection, courage, and something she couldn't quite define. She looked up at him through her bangs.

"When are you going to yell at me?" he asked. She led them toward the cushioned wicker bench and motioned for him to sit down. She scooched to the corner.

"How can I yell, when I'm relieved, you're here? Plus, Sarah's been saying for almost two weeks that I should expect you. She laughed at me after I called you, she said it was an engraved invitation."

He scowled at her. "It wasn't. I really had to think this over. But after imbibing a tall, cool can of fuck-it-all, I decided this was the right thing to do."

She giggled.

"I've been around a lot of military men, and I haven't heard about that drink yet."

"I'm thinking of starting a home brewery."

He held out his hand, palm up. She looked at it. Then she looked at him, his face, his smile, his eyes. She still didn't take his outstretched hand.

"You know we've never even kissed. This makes no

sense whatsoever." Even to her own ears, it was a weak protest.

He didn't say anything, just kept his hand out.

"Where do we go from here?"

He continued his silence and still offered his hand.

Dammit!

She might visit war-torn countries and not know what was going to come at her when, but she was a doctor; she thrived on order in her personal life. She wanted control. She loved plans and precision. She wanted a *damn* road map! With a warranty!

"Carys, take my hand," he whispered.

His voice could talk the birds from the trees or sing a newborn baby to sleep. She wanted to listen to that voice forever. How was that possible? She'd only known him for five days.

Carys looked at his hand one last time and pushed it out of her way as she launched herself at him. She wound her arms around his neck. It was awkward at first as she came at him sideways, but of course he fixed it. He always made things better. Soon, he had her cuddled in his lap and she was looking up at him.

She grabbed at his short black hair, trying to force his head down. She wanted her kiss.

His smile was wicked. "This is our first kiss, Woman. It's going to be spectacular. You're not going to get me to rush my fences."

Now she pulled at his hair, trying to hurt him, the jerk. He chuckled.

He brushed at the new bangs that fluttered against

her forehead. "You've changed your hair. Do you like it?"

She swallowed. "I do," she whispered. "I used to really love playing with different cuts and styles, but I lost that. Now I have that back."

"God, you're gorgeous. I don't care if your hair is loose, in a braid, or shaved off. You are beautiful to me."

He was going to make her cry. She believed him.

She tugged on his hair again, trying to tempt him downwards. He laughed.

He slid his fingers through the hair at the base of her skull and she arched into the feel. As she was luxuriating in his touch, Cullen feathered a kiss along her jaw.

No!

That wasn't what she wanted. It wasn't what she needed.

She turned her head, trying to catch his lips, and then he was there gracing her with the softest kiss imaginable as their lips met for the first time.

arys.

Carys.

She'd been haunting his dreams. His life had been colorless for the last goddamn month as he'd sat waiting for any kind of communication, and now...

Now...

He sifted his fingers through the fine silk of her red-gold hair, softly, wanting to infuse the caress with only pleasure. She arched into his touch, and that's when he went in for more. Her lips beckoned, he needed to taste them again.

Don't get greedy.

Slow.

He met her mouth with a slow slide of his own, and she moaned. Her plump lips softened against his and little by little she opened for him. Cullen was getting into this. He was wooing her response. He feathered his tongue along her bottom lip, she tasted like sunshine. Her lips caught his tongue, and then she snipped at it with her teeth.

He let out a long groan.

She let go and looked up at him with wide green eyes. "Was that a good groan?"

"Let's experiment ten more times and find out," he suggested.

A smile blossomed on her face. "Let's."

She cupped his smooth cheeks, and then trailed her fingers along the side of his jaw. "I can't decide," she said. There was a twinkle in her eye, but he could also see a soul-deep well of desire. She was just as needy as he was.

"What can't you decide?" he asked.

"If I like the scruff from Africa, or this smooth urbane look that you're sporting here in the States."

He winced. "I'm kind of hoping you like smooth twice a week, and whiskers five days a week."

She drew back.

"You see us together a lot, don't you?"

"You're not in Eugene. Where do you want to be? Here? Because I have a proposition for you. I want us to date. I want to go out to dinner with you, I want movies, maybe popcorn and wine on the couch while we watch shitty cable TV shows, and I bring you flowers."

"Wine?" She lifted her eyebrow.

"Okay, beer for me, or better yet, Fanta. And I have a plan on how we can do all of this."

"What's your plan?"

"It's easy and manageable."

She shifted so she could sit up a little more. Cullen winced, because she was wiggling on his hard-on.

"Oh!" Carys said as she figured out what was going on. "I'm sorry. I didn't mean..."

"Honey, if you were in my lap and I wasn't aroused, we'd have a problem."

Damn, for a doctor, she sure was naïve.

She wiggled one more time and arranged her ass on his thigh instead of on his dick. "Okay, that's better," she said after having turned one-hundred shades of pink. "Now what, Oh-Mighty-SEAL, is your plan?"

"Come to Virginia with me. I *also* have a guest bedroom. As a matter of a fact, I have *two* kitted out, so you'll have a choice. I would suggest you use the one that Chelle uses. The one that Baily uses is often taken over by Aries no matter what I try to do to dissuade him."

"Hmmm, so you just hit me with a lot, Cullen. Move to Virginia—"

"Eventually move," he interrupted. "Visit to begin with."

"Okay, visit. Then there's Chelle, Baily, and Aries. Who are they?"

"Sister. Sister. Dog."

She gave him an arch look. "Again. That's a lot."

"Which parts?"

"Surprisingly, it's the sister, sister, and dog. I'm liking the part where I come out for a visit. Not necessarily staying with you. I can stay at a hotel."

Don't grin.

Do. Not. Grin.

"A hotel won't work," he said in a teasing tone. "I'm still going to have to be at the base most weekdays, and then you'll be bored during the day without my smiling face around and you stuck in some gloomy hotel. But, if you're at my place you can acclimate yourself to the area. I can also introduce you to some great people and you can spend some time with the sister, sister, and dog."

"Cullen—"

He propped her up, so they were nose-to-nose and he smiled. "Now, let me be serious for a second. Remember what I said about not wanting to rush my fences?"

After a moment, she nodded.

"In no way, shape, or form do I want to push you into anything you're not ready for. Coax you? Cajole you? Absolutely. But I don't even want to try to seduce you, Carys. This is all on your timeline. You've been hurt, I know this. I want a chance for you to get to know me when we're not running for our lives through Africa."

"That's not the part that scares me," she whispered.

"What is?" *What have I missed?*

"What happens when you finally get to know the real me?" she asked.

He cupped her soft cheek and traced her plump satin soft bottom lip. "Then I will fall even harder."

∼

Pulling herself out of his arms had been a heck of a lot harder than she thought it should be. Apparently, it wasn't just newborns that needed skin-to-skin contact. Carys blushed as she thought about lip-to-lip contact.

Sarah caught her from across the table and raised her eyebrow. Darn it. It was tough having such a good friend that they could read your mind. Sarah had been trying to drag her into the back bedroom ever since she and Cullen had come back into the dining room for dinner. Carys had avoided the girl chat. Part of it was because she didn't know what to say, but if she were truly honest, the real reason was that she didn't want to miss a moment of her time with Cullen. And, drat it, Sarah seemed to have guessed that too!

"Aunt Carys, who drew this?" Tonya asked as she held up a well-executed drawing in pencil on lined paper. It showed a mother holding a baby. Carys looked down at the corner of the paper.

"A little girl named Leila drew that," she answered Tonya. "I met her a while ago. She lives with her mother, sisters, and brother in Egypt."

"How'd you get it?" The little girl's piping voice brought back visions of the two girls in Sudan.

"Mr. Lyons brought the pictures and letter to me when he came to visit. Wasn't that nice of him?"

"Uh-huh," Tonya nodded vigorously.

"Do you want to see pictures of Leila and her sister?" Cullen asked.

"Can I, Mom?" Tonya asked as she slipped off her chair in preparation for her mother's affirmative answer. As soon as she got the nod, she ran around the table to the side where Cullen and Carys sat. Cullen had his phone out, and Tonya immediately hung over his arm to check out the pictures.

"Where was that? Is that Egypt?"

"Nope, that's Sudan, but both of those countries are on the continent of Africa," Cullen explained.

"They're pretty," Tonya said. "I like her braids." Cullen didn't seem to mind the little girl's fingerprints on his phone.

"Dad, can we go to the continental of Africa? Can I have my hair braided, Mom?"

"It's the continent of Africa, not continental, Honey," David corrected. "And we're visiting your grandparents first." David turned to his wife and tugged on her hair. "You're up, champ."

"I'll braid your hair tomorrow," she promised her daughter.

"Coolness. Aunt Carys, can I draw a picture for Leila?"

"You sure can," she said. "Now, where are those brownies you helped bake?"

"I'll get 'em," Tonya said with a huge grin that was missing some teeth.

"How about I help?" David stood up and followed his daughter into the kitchen.

"Your kid is a doll," Cullen said as he leaned in to hand his phone to Sarah who'd been motioning for it.

Carys sat back in her chair and let everything after that just wash over her. She'd been here with Sarah, David, and Tonya for five weeks and it had really helped. Sarah was her best friend and she'd let her cry and scream when needed as she dealt with the agony of losing so many of her team members. She'd been the same woman who had helped put her partially back together after Santa Flores.

David and Tonya made a flourish out of the ice cream that went with the brownies, and Cullen and David bonded over shared military experiences. The way that David ended up braiding Tonya's hair while he talked to Cullen melted Carys' heart. When she tried to help with the clean-up, Sarah gently shoved her back into the seat next to Cullen.

Is this how my life could be? Isn't it about time I took the risk?

"Are you sure your guy really works for the Army?" Cullen asked David. "He's sounding like the same guy named Kevin we have working for us at Little Creek. Mouth-breather, right? Can't follow an order to save his life?"

"That's the guy. But he's ours—I know it because I'm the one who filled out his last fitness report. You know, the one that got him demoted," David laughed as he sat back and parted out his daughter's hair.

"Don't lie to me, you didn't demote him, you transferred him to us," Cullen laughed.

He has a great laugh.

Sarah winked at her.

Carys wasn't all that surprised when the little Sloane family went to bed and left her to wave Cullen on his way. Heck, if she knew her friend Sarah, she was hoping the man would spend the night.

They sat on the couch in the living room drinking milk and indulging in another brownie.

"Did you think about my great idea?" Cullen asked. "Great, huh?"

"Grand? Stupendous? Fan-tab-u-lous?"

She sat close with his arm around her. It felt so good, and so right. The idea of having this while staying at his house in Virginia was seductive.

She heard the sound of *Frère Jacques,* and realized her phone was ringing. It was the ring tone she rarely heard. It was Marie-Clare.

"What is it?" Cullen asked when Carys got up from the couch to go to the kitchen where her phone was charging.

"It's Marie-Clair Peirot. She's the psychologist I worked with at the refugee camp in Greece." She quirked an eyebrow at Cullen when he took the moment to snag two more brownies as she answered her phone.

"Hello," she said in French.

"Hello," Marie-Clair responded in kind. "I have bad news. I hate having to deliver it over the phone but I'm in Lebanon and I have no way of getting to you in person."

"Slow down, Marie-Claire, you know my French isn't that good," Carys said, concerned. "Are you all right?"

"Me, I am fine."

Carys breathed a sigh of relief. "Is it any of our former teammates?" She didn't think she could take it if more doctors and nurses had been killed.

"No, no, no. They're all right. It is little Raviq."

With those few words, Carys' blood ran cold. She

thought of the little boy from the refugee camp in Greece the way she had last seen him. His blue shirt that barely covered his tummy, his sullen expression, the way he hadn't even cried at his own father's farce of a funeral. Marie-Claire was going to say he was dead.

"He's in Canada with his mom, right?" Carys said desperately.

"No, my love, he's not. His visa got denied at the last moment. He ended up in another refugee camp. This time in Lebanon."

"Tell me," Carys begged. "Just tell me what happened."

"He was found next to the security fence. Dead. I don't have the particulars. They just told me he was in bad shape when they found him. I don't know if that means he was close to death already or if he was killed."

Marie-Claire's voice shook. Carys wanted to comfort her, she did. But she couldn't. The woman kept talking. She couldn't understand anymore. It was like a switch had shut off in Carys' mind. She pulled the phone away from her ear. Then it fell from her nerveless fingers.

I need her to stop talking.

Vaguely, she heard Cullen talking on the phone. She didn't know what he was saying, she didn't care. As long as she didn't have to hear Marie-Claire anymore.

"Honey?"

She couldn't see. She didn't want to hear.

Where am I?

She opened her eyes and realized her head was

between her knees, she was staring at the floor, her back was against the floor cupboards. Sarah and David's house?

"Carys? Can you speak to me?"

I don't want to talk.

"Okay, you don't have to, Baby. I'm just going to sit next to you."

She didn't respond. How could she? Life wasn't real. Nothing was. *Please say nothing is real.*

She heard more than felt her sob.

Raviq. Oh God, poor little Raviq with the most sorrowful brown eyes. He's dead. Dead in a ditch in some Goddamn refugee camp in Lebanon when he was supposed to be in Canada.

"Cullen, why wasn't he in Canada? I don't understand?"

Carys shuddered.

"I don't know, Baby."

She tried to get up from the floor, but when she pushed up, her hand slipped, and she crashed back down.

"Let me help you. I don't want you hurt." She felt Cullen try to help her up.

"It's okay," she sobbed. "I'm not hurt. Raviq is hurt," she tried to explain. Then in her mind's eye she saw Raviq's brown eyes and started crying even harder.

"Okay, we'll just stay here." Strong arms pulled her into a hug.

"He died," she wailed. "They killed him. All those fucking bastards killed him."

She buried her face into his neck and wept. It

wasn't enough, so she pulled him closer. She remembered Raviq letting her wash his face and hands and give him some soup. He was missing a tooth, but she only saw it once because he'd only smiled once.

Cullen?

"I'm here, Carys. I'm not going anywhere." Had she said his name out loud?

"That little baby boy went through so much. Why did this happen?" she begged him and the universe for an answer.

"Tell me!" she screamed.

Cullen didn't flinch. He pulled her in even closer.

"Raviq!"

~

Cullen wasn't surprised when David and Sarah came into the kitchen. They took in the scene and Sarah rushed over and crouched in front of Carys.

"Sweetheart, what's wrong?"

"Raviq is dead."

"The little boy from the refugee camp?" her friend asked.

Carys nodded, not lifting her head from Cullen's neck.

"Oh, Carys, I'm so sorry. Can I get you something? Some tea?"

He felt Carys flinch and snuggle even closer to him.

"Sarah, I think Cullen's got this, let's go to bed," David said.

Sarah reached out and touched Carys' shoulder. "Do you need me to do anything? Anything at all?"

"No," Carys whimpered.

"Come on, Babe," David said again. "Let's go check on Tonya."

He watched over Carys' head as David gave him a chin tilt, then guided his wife out of the kitchen. He turned off the overhead light, leaving the room lit just by the stove light. Carys continued to shudder in his arms. He understood now—it was the boy she'd cared about in Greece, the one who had tried to kill himself. Cullen's heart hurt for the boy, but it was breaking for Carys. She tried so hard and kept so much inside herself.

She shifted. It was time to get somewhere comfortable.

Cullen swooped her up into his arms and strode into the living room and settled her onto his lap. He brushed the hair away from her wet face. Tears started to form again, and his heart clenched.

Carys' arms twined around his neck and held on for dear life.

When he heard hiccoughs, he asked, "do you want to talk about him?"

She nodded.

"I need—"

He reached across her body and snagged some napkins off the coffee table from their brownie feast. She clutched one in her hand, then she blew her nose.

"He was a beautiful boy, so angry, but you understood why. He was infinitely loveable."

Cullen nodded and continued to roam her back with long strokes, encouraging her to tell him more.

"Marie-Clare had told me how they'd gotten visas to go to Canada. I was so happy for them. Nobody deserved it more."

Again, Cullen didn't say anything, just gave her a nod and a half-smile to continue. "Tonight, she didn't tell me what went wrong, just that they ended up in a refugee camp in Lebanon. That would have been his worst nightmare. They found him dead," she said the last words with chattering teeth. "She didn't know the cause of death." The last she said on a low wail.

"Ah, Baby."

"I'm so sick of not making a difference. The needless devastation and pain. It's not fair." She hit his chest. "It's just not fair."

"No, Carys, it isn't."

No sobs this time, just a trickle of tears.

Cullen gathered her close and started to rock her. He didn't know how long they did this, but eventually she slept.

19

*I*t was dawn when Carys woke up in Cullen's arms. She almost felt good. How was that even possible considering the fact that Raviq was dead? She looked down and realized it was because of the man beneath her. He had let her cry her eyes out and kept her safe.

She pictured Raviq's one smile and held it close in her heart. Then she sent up a prayer.

You beautiful boy. Please be in God's arms and be at peace. I love you.

She breathed a sigh of pleasure and looked down at Cullen. It was a rare occurrence for her to get a chance to study the man at rest. He was a wonderful man. How had she gotten so lucky to have a man who was willing to track her down?

His eyes opened.

"Good morning, Honey." And that wonderful growly voice. She could just roll around in it like a cat in catnip.

"Is that invite to Virginia still open?" she asked.

All sleepiness disappeared from his eyes.

"Of course it is. Even more today than yesterday."

"Why? That makes no sense. You just saw me have a total meltdown. If anything, you should be scared."

"Are you kidding? Your level of caring, love, and empathy just makes me want you more, Carys."

She was stunned.

"But, Cullen, what if I let you down?" she voiced her biggest fear. "I'm not sure I'm up for the physical side of a relationship." She stared at his chest, unable to meet his eyes. He put a finger under her chin and tilted her head upward, forcing her to meet his eyes.

"We just take it one day at a time, it's all anyone can do. But the woman I think I've come to know is probably tired of the stasis she's in. Am I right?"

He was.

"I want more from life. But I don't want you to think I'm using you."

He laughed. It was a big laugh and she was afraid he might wake her friends. "Use me. I'm begging you."

"You're a nutbar."

"Yes, I am. Want to take a bite?" He got up from the couch and picked up their dishes from last night. "It's time to say good-night."

"It's morning," she pointed out.

"I still want you to sleep on it. Get some real shut-eye. Then call me when you wake up. I want to make sure you mean it when I get a 'Yes' from you."

She followed him into the kitchen as she rolled her eyes. God, the man oozed confidence.

At least one of us does.

He held her hand as they walked to the door. Even that little bit of touch turned her on. Okay, so the physical side of a relationship was probably not going to be a problem.

"Ready for a good-morning kiss?" he asked.

"Oh, yes."

He folded her into his arms and she melted into his strength and warmth. Once again, he started with those light, coaxing kisses.

"Harder."

"We'll get there, but not now when I'm about to leave."

His tongue traced her bottom lip, soft and beguiling, she followed his lead and enjoyed every minute of the journey. She was dizzy with desire. His arm pulled her closer, and a warm hand snuck beneath her sweater and drizzled waves of heat on top of long dormant nerve endings. She shivered and pressed closer.

Carys clutched at his shirt, distantly realizing her nails were digging into his chest, but she didn't care. He should be punished for putting her through this much pleasure and pain.

How can I ache this badly?

He trailed kisses along her jaw and licked her collar bone. He was kneading her scalp, helping her come down off her physical high.

"Don't leave," she entreated.

He brushed back her hair and stared at her with solemn blue eyes. "I have to leave. I promised not to seduce you. It's too soon for this, Carys, and deep down you know it. You need to know me better."

She sighed. "I *know* you, Cullen. I just want to know *us*."

"There's my smart doctor."

"I'm going to take you to lunch later today. We can discuss your future plans then, okay?" He held her hand, his thumb brushed over the Claddagh ring on her pinkie.

"Okay," she agreed. "I want waffles."

"For lunch? Do you know a place that serves waffles for lunch?"

"Yep."

"With strawberries?" he asked.

"Blackberries. And homemade whipped cream."

She gripped his hand tight.

"This is a good thing, Carys. I promise."

"I know," she lied.

He chuckled, and she knew that he saw through her lie. Cullen opened the door and stepped out onto the stoop. "I'll be waiting for your call, now get your tushie to bed. Don't forget to lock up after me."

She nodded, then did just that. She watched out the side window as he walked past the trike on the way to the rental car. By God, she was going to reach for the brass ring. She might not get it, but at least she will have tried.

~

Love me, love my dog.

Cullen had always believed in that saying, but seriously? Carys had been playing with Aries for twenty-six minutes. It was twenty-four minutes too damn long as far as he was concerned. Her red-gold hair shone in the afternoon light as she played tug-o-war with the knotted rope in his backyard with his rambunctious German Shephard. Aries would keep at this for another two hours if he let him. But enough was enough already.

He gave a command whistle and Aries dropped the toy, sending Carys on her cute little jeans-clad ass. Aries high-tailed it over to him on his deck.

"Hey, I call foul," Carys called up to him.

"Dinner's going to burn pretty soon."

She got up and brushed off her butt and grinned as she sauntered up the hill to his house. "Well, why didn't you say so?"

"I've already called out twice, you ignored me. Apparently, Aries minds better."

"He's a good dog," Carys agreed as she got to the top of the stairs. "So, what did you make?"

"Spaghetti, garlic bread, and asparagus."

"I've got to clean up," she said as she looked down at her clothes.

"That's why I called you in early." He opened the door to the house and followed her in.

She'd just arrived two hours ago, which had given her enough time to choose a room, store her stuff, get a drink, and then become best friends with his dog.

"You have a beautiful house," she said again.

"The basement still needs some work. Zed was

going to help me, but he's still not in any shape to do construction."

In some of their phone calls over the last three weeks, Cullen had filled her in on all his teammates, including Zed Zaragoza, the man who had almost died in one of their last missions.

"When am I going to meet him?" Carys asked as she took the glass of lemonade that Cullen offered her.

"I'm throwing you into the deep end tomorrow. We're going over to a party at Kane's house. He's even invited my demon sisters, so you're in for a wild ride."

Cullen watched her carefully to see if there was any kind apprehension on her face, but if anything, she looked excited at the prospect.

"Let me grab a shower, and I'll come set the table," she smiled. He watched her walk down the short hallway to her room, then turned to go to the kitchen. Aries of course had followed Carys, he was a smart and traitorous dog.

His phone rang and he picked it up as he stirred the sauce.

"Is she here? Can we come over?"

"Yes, she's here. No, you can't come over. Don't even think about it. I've already set the alarm."

"Come on, are you denying your baby sister? You love me," Baily whined.

"You'll meet her tomorrow, at Kane's house."

He heard her sigh through the phone. "You're a party-pooper."

"That has to be the least foul thing you've ever called me, Baily. Things are looking up in my world."

"Asshole."

Cullen laughed as he hung up on his sister.

Carys pulled on the black skinny jeans and scooped neck sweater that she'd bought on a shopping trip with Sarah. Apparently, the effort was worth it by the gleam in Cullen's eye when he spotted her walking into the kitchen.

"Hey, Beautiful."

"Hi. How can I help?"

"I've got everything ready to go. You just have to tell me what you'd like to drink. I have Chianti, water, all kinds of juices, or pineapple Fanta."

He pulled out the Fanta from the fridge as he was talking and she grinned as she snatched it from him. She cuddled it close to her as she walked to the kitchen nook where the table was set.

"Hope you don't mind, I don't eat in the formal dining room all that often unless I'm having a bunch of people over."

"This suits me perfectly. If you give me a Fanta, I'm good in the back of a truck, too."

Cullen motioned for her to help herself to the food, and she grabbed some pasta, sauce, vegetables, and bread. She looked over to where Aries sat upright.

"He's not begging," she noted.

"He knows the rules. If he plays by them, then he gets a snack." Cullen handed her a glass filled with ice for her soda. She took it and filled her glass with the sweet pineapple goodness. She could get used to this kind of care, she'd just need to make sure she could provide it back.

"I don't cook," she blurted out, after she finished a bite of spaghetti.

Cullen looked up from his plate. "Good to know."

"Well, I can, a little. I mean grilled cheese sandwiches. I could cook spaghetti, but not the sauce, unless it came from a jar. Did it?"

Cullen shook his head.

"It didn't? How'd you make it?"

"Mom's recipe. It's really pretty simple. You put the first set of ingredients from Mom's recipe in a thick pot on the stove until the meat is browned and the vegetables are tender, then you stir in the rest of the stuff on the recipe and bring to a boil. You really can't fuck it up."

Carys set down her fork and stared at Cullen in amazement. "You do realize you're scaring the heck out of me. I've screwed up every single recipe that Sarah or Peter has ever had me try to make. I've managed to screw up boxed macaroni and cheese. Apparently, you're not supposed to put in the entire packet of cheese because then it gets too cheesy. Tell me, why would they give you that much cheese, if you're not supposed to use it?"

Cullen laughed. "So, you're telling me that while you're visiting, you're not going to be cooking?"

"I can do laundry. I like things very clean. I use a lot of bleach."

"That would be the doctor in you coming out," he teased. "Do you use bleach on your unmentionables?"

Carys blushed thinking about the new underwear that Sarah had talked her into purchasing. She sure wasn't going to bleach all those lacy bits of froth, not after what she spent on them.

"Tell me why you're blushing," Cullen prompted.

"It must be that I'm suffering from low blood sugar. I need to eat." She forked in some asparagus, so she didn't have to answer. Cullen continued to laugh.

"Carys, why are you worried about not being able to cook and saying you can do laundry. This isn't a competition."

"I just want to be able to pull my weight."

"Well, first of all, you weigh a hell of a lot less than I do, so you don't have to pull as much."

She glared at him.

"Second, you're staying at my place as my guest, so right now, I'm doing things for you."

She continued to glare at him.

"Third, I like doing for you."

"Cullen, I'd like to do things for you too. We would need to be equal in this, if this relationship were to work."

"Hot damn, you said relationship!" he shouted.

Aries stood up and barked.

"Oh God, you're both against me," Carys moaned and covered her face. She couldn't decide if it was funny or scary or both.

"Nope, we're both on your side."

She heard the scrape of a chair, and Cullen was

beside her pulling down her hands. "Look at me, Sweetheart."

She looked up at him and smiled. He really was a wonderful man. "I did say relationship, didn't I?"

~

She was such a dichotomy, Cullen thought to himself. Shy sometimes, and balls-out gutsy at other times. He never knew what he was going to get with this woman. But apparently, he wasn't going to get a cook.

"You're smiling. Why are you smiling?" she asked.

"I'm trying to take things slow, Carys, but it's damn hard. Literally."

She giggled, an actual girlish giggle. Wasn't that one of the best sounds in the world?

Can I tell her yet?

Cullen muffled his sigh. Any talk of love would probably have her running for the hills. He needed to do more groundwork. But preparation was his middle name. He glanced over and saw that she'd finished dinner.

"I've got a lemon merengue pie for dessert. You interested?" he asked.

"Please don't say you can bake, too. I'm begging you."

"Store-bought, I promise."

"Thank God. But not right now." Her voice was a low whisper.

"Okay, let's go out onto the deck and watch the sunset."

She nodded. He pulled her up from her seat and guided her outside. He'd bought the slider swing last week when she'd agreed to come out for a visit. He'd even arranged the soft afghan throw with her in mind. He'd been imagining many nights of them snuggling under the Chesapeake night sky as she got more and more comfortable with him.

The last week he'd been working in Africa, he'd spent some time with Jack Preston of the Midnight Delta team. At one point, Jack had been assigned to the Black Dawn Navy SEAL team who had been in Santa Flores. It was Jack who'd burst into the room where Carys had been held captive. He'd been there the moment she'd shoved a knife into the man who'd been brutally abusing her.

Jack told Cullen all about that scene. Cullen thought he was going to throw up when the big Texan told him the gory details, but instead he listened to every word. Up to that point, he'd been blown away by the good doctor, her strength and heart were second to none. But after hearing that story, he was in awe of her personal courage. The fact that Carys would continue to put herself in harm's way and not grow a hard shell as she dealt with others made him fall in love even deeper.

"This glides," she smiled at him as she sat down.

"Wanted to outdo David," Cullen said.

"No, you didn't, you're not competitive like that," Carys protested.

Cullen snorted. She was such a naïve little thing.

He covered them with the throw, and she nestled up

close to his side, making it easy for him to put his arm around her. She fit perfectly.

Cullen sifted his fingers through the fine silk of her hair. "Why'd you decide to start wearing your hair loose?" he asked.

She snuggled closer. He felt her breath against the nape of his neck as she answered. "Part of me felt really scared after I came home from Africa. Losing so many members of my team and Joyce like I did, it broke my heart." Cullen tugged her closer and she sighed. He waited for her to continue.

"But some things weren't as scary. Like when David hugged me, or when my hair came loose. It was weird, but some part of me started waking up again, and seemed to be healing. I was getting over some of my old fear."

Cullen didn't ask her why that might have been happening. Instead he waited for her to continue.

Please let her continue.

"Even though you and I were together only three days, I felt like I could trust again. Cullen, you did that for me."

"No, Sweetheart, you were always going to get there. There is nothing you're not capable of, your strength astounds me."

Her head shot up so fast that it hit his chin.

"Oh my God, I'm so sorry, did I hurt you?"

"I'm fine, Carys," he assured her. He pulled her head down so he could rub the top of it. "Are you hurt?" he asked.

"I'm fine. But do you know how good it makes me

feel, to hear you say you think I'm strong? I've been feeling so weak and broken for so long, and it feels wonderful to finally be back in the driver's seat."

"Are you saying you were feeling weak in Africa?"

She paused, then looked up at him with her big green eyes. "Well, yes," she admitted.

"Well, God help me, if that's you being weak, I'm in for a world of trouble."

"Yes, I think you might be," her smile was a sight to behold.

This time, he couldn't start with a slow kiss, it just wasn't possible, and thank God, she seemed to be on the same page as him. When Cullen dipped his head, she raised her lips in response and it was electric. Her mouth flowered open for the thrust of his tongue.

Her nails scraped his jaw. No woman had ever done that before. It felt crazy good. He opened his eyes and found her staring at him. He broke the kiss.

"No. Don't stop."

"Are you scared? Am I coming on too strong?"

"Don't second guess anything," she said fiercely. "I want this. I want to savor every second. You feel so good." Her palm rubbed up his cheek, her fingers tangled into his hair and tried to pull him downwards.

"You like pulling my hair, don't you?"

She frowned. "I guess I do. How odd."

Ooops. "No overthinking, Carys, we're into the feels." He moved his hand from around her back and coaxed her up onto his lap, so that she was straddling him. He saw a look of satisfaction cross her face. He'd been hoping she would like being in a position of power. All in all, he could kind of understand why pulling *his* hair might bring her a sense of satisfaction as well.

"Be prepared to be ravished," she purred.

I'm in trouble now.

20

*C*arys felt like she was soaring. This was better than any dessert she had ever had in her life. Cullen was all hard, tantalizing muscle and he smelled so good. He tasted good. The only thing soft about him were his eyes and lips. Those lips. Somebody should write a poem about his lips.

"Carys, stop staring and kiss me or touch me or something."

That voice.

"Carys," he growled.

So low and gravelly. She felt it in the pit of her stomach.

He grabbed her around her waist and dragged her down, so their lips met.

Sublime.

Kissing and kissing and kissing. She was losing herself in a whirlwind of sensation as his hands stroked her neck, her shoulders, trailing down her spine and finally those powerful hands molded her butt and she about lost her mind.

What mind?

She whimpered as she tried to get her hands under his shirt, but her body was in the way.

"Baby, what is it?"

"I want to feel you," she wailed as she tried tugging again at the front of his sweater. Then she sighed in relief as she worked around to his back and lifted it up and felt the smooth, taut, muscled skin of his back. He felt so good.

The afghan slipped onto the deck. "Honey, we have to take this inside, are you good with that?"

She peppered kisses up the side of his neck, her tongue licking up the taste of him. "Oh yes, inside. Hurry, Cullen." She struggled to get up.

He flexed his muscles and her eyes went wide as she found herself in his arms as he stood up on the deck. "You're not supposed to be able to do that."

"Carys, we kind of do a lot of physical training in my job," he chuckled as he tucked one arm under her bottom and easily opened the door to the house.

Strong is good. I like strong.

She melted against him, secure in the knowledge that he would take care of her. She didn't pay any attention as to where they were going. She continued to stroke the warm heat of his back and lick the sweet and salty skin of his neck.

Her world dipped and she found herself on her back.

"Are you okay, Sweetheart?"

"Why wouldn't I be?"

Cullen traced the contours of her face with his fingers, as he stared down at her. Then she realized he was worried.

"I've never felt so safe, or so aroused," she confessed.

"That's good, because nothing in my life has ever felt as good as this moment."

He meant it, she could see it in his eyes. Carys blinked fast, not wanting to ruin the moment with tears. Now was a time of joy.

With his eyes on hers, he lowered his head and their lips met. Kiss after kiss and she was once again lost in a maelstrom of desire. When his lips left hers, she realized her top was gone and he had moved to brush his tongue across her over-sensitive nipple.

Her back arched so far off the bed she thought she might break in half. So good, it was glorious.

"More."

Was that my voice?

Cullen's mouth surrounded the tip of her breast and he lashed at her with his tongue. Vaguely she heard her whimpers of pleasure. She wanted to tell him not to stop. She wanted to beg him for something more because she was coming apart, but she couldn't make words form. She tried to lift her hands to guide him, but they wouldn't work.

She watched through slitted eyes as he pulled off her jeans and panties. Every nerve in her body tingled, and she felt every rub of cloth. Her skin was too sensitive. It was all too much. It wasn't enough.

"God, you're gorgeous," he breathed.

Say something.

"Take…" She languidly lifted one arm.

"What, Honey?"

"You now."

He bent over her, his clothes rasping along her tender skin.

"What do you want, Carys?"

"You. Naked. Now."

Cullen's laugh was throaty. She shivered as it hit every erogenous zone in her body.

Don't lose it now, Lyons.

She shoved at his sweater collar with a whine of frustration. He knelt up on the bed and ripped it up over his head and threw it onto the floor. Her hand reached for the button of his jeans, but he wasn't having it. A man needed a little bit of time and space to accomplish all his goals.

"Nuh-uh," he admonished, as he gently pushed her hands away. He was careful not to grab her wrists or do anything to restrain her. When she tried again, he leaned forward for another deep, lush, long kiss. He'd had dreams about her lips, not one of them had come even close to reality.

He rubbed his chest hair against the hard tips of her breasts as he continued to savor the heady rush that came from kissing Carys Adams. She filled the missing place in his heart, and he couldn't get enough of her. He combed his fingers through her beautiful hair and loved the way it spilled across his pillow.

I have her. She's finally in my bed.

Her hands rested beside her head now, and Cullen traced his fingertips from her palms down to her collarbone. Then he trailed farther down to her gorgeous, delicately formed breasts and traced circles around her areolas. Carys' breathing turned harsh and her head began to toss side to side. He sucked a nipple into his mouth while lightly tugging on the other.

She drew in a deep breath then groaned.

"Carys?"

"Oh, yes. I like this."

Thank God.

He continued to lave and lick her tender nub, as his other hand trailed down her stomach to reach the damp curls. Carys parted her legs, but as soon as his fingers touched her sex, she clamped her legs closed on his hand, holding him captive exactly where he wanted to be. Cullen was nobody's fool. He took advantage.

He moved his head up and rested his forehead against hers so he could look into green eyes dark with desire. Then he moved two fingers ever so slowly against her tender, wet flesh. Her eyes grew wide and she licked her lips. He continued his languid strokes for long minutes until she gradually relaxed.

Thank ever loving fuck he'd left his jeans on, otherwise he would have lost it by now.

"Cullen?"

"Right here, Baby," he rasped.

Her thighs parted. "I need you."

With one finger he tested her depth.

Damn, she was so tight. "Soon."

"No, now." She lifted up and kissed his neck, his jaw, then captured his lips. He was lost...almost. He kept up with a rhythm. One finger, then as she melted around him, two fingers. She sighed, then arched.

"Please Cullen."

I love you. I love you so much. Please let me get this right.

He stood up and shucked his jeans. He grabbed a condom from his nightstand and looked down at the most beautiful woman in the world. Her green eyes glittered up at him, her smile was a sultry temptation.

She lifted a knee and he caressed it, stroking down toward her ankle. Her toes curled and then she lifted her foot up and up until it glided down his hip.

"God," he shuddered. "Are you trying to kill me?"

"Tempt you," she purred.

He loved it. "Oh, you're doing that all right." He looked at her face, then his eyes were drawn to the pink folds of her sex. It was as if she were made for him. He had to touch her one last time, feel her response.

When his thumb brushed against the swollen nub of her clit, her moan turned into a muffled shriek of want as she covered her mouth. She was so close.

Perfect.

He pulled her closer to the edge of the bed and positioned the head of his cock to her tight opening. He tried desperately to hold onto his control, so that he could watch her reactions as he experienced the most profound pleasure of his life.

Her legs circled his waist, her heels digging into his ass, thrusting upwards, driving him deep.

"Yes," she gasped. Her body convulsed. "Oh yes, Cullen." Her head thrashed, her eyes a dark emerald green. She reached out with her hands, beckoning him.

Exactly. He needed to hold her. He sank down on top of her and she sighed in pleasure, curving her body to meet his. He kissed her, needing her taste, needing to be surrounded and connected in all ways as he began to thrust in and out of the slick heat of her body.

She matched him perfectly. There wasn't one move he made that she didn't echo, not one need he had that she didn't meet.

Her panting turned to gasps and he opened his eyes to watch her. She bit her nails into his back, hard. He loved it.

"Cullen." She stammered his name.

"Right here." He kissed her jaw and thrust deep, knowing exactly what she needed.

Her breathing turned ragged. She opened her mouth, and nothing came out but a whine.

"Now, Sweetheart, I've got you."

Her eyes opened and he saw more than her moment of bliss, he saw joy, as they both hurled past the stars.

Ah, God, there they were, the Demon Sisters. He pulled Carys tighter to his side.

"What?" she asked as she looked up at him. Once

again, she was drinking a pineapple Fanta that he had brought with them to Kane's party.

"My sisters have arrived."

"They have? Is that them?" She looked out the window to the driveway below. "Let's go help them. They have their hands full." Carys sounded like a little kid at Christmas.

"I'm sure the guys will be there in a second." Cullen saw that his premonition was correct. Leo, Asher, and Nick were outside in a second and on his sisters like a bad case of poison ivy.

"On second thought, let's go help."

Carys snickered.

"Oh, you think you're so smart," he said as he guided her through a throng of people to the front door.

"Yes, I do. I went to medical school, there were psychology courses."

Before they got to the door, Baily and Chelle were inside and greeted by a chorus of 'hello's'.

Leo, Nick, and Asher followed with bags and dishes of food.

"They can cook too, I see."

"Chelle can," Cullen said. "The grocery bags are probably filled with alcohol, chips, and mixer. That will be Baily's contribution."

"A girl after my own heart."

"Where is she?" Baily called out.

Cullen winced. Seriously, his little sister needed to gain a sense of decorum.

"She's talking about me, isn't she?" Carys asked.

Cullen heard the first little bit of trepidation in her voice and he was going to kick Baily's ass.

"Wait, I see her," Baily grinned as she pushed Baby Nick out of her way.

"Hi, Carys, I brought more Fanta! I also made Mom bake lemon tarts. You're going to be in heaven."

Carys looked up at him and blushed. Cullen was immediately in her head and he damn near blushed as well, remembering yesterday evening, last night, and this morning. Dear God, the woman had rocked his world.

Chelle walked up at that point. "Did you tell them about Mom's lemon tarts?" she asked Baily.

"Yeah, but Cullen started thinking about sex." Baily rolled her eyes.

"Interesting," Chelle answered. She gave Cullen a droll look. But he was happy to see that both of his sisters focused on him and weren't giving Carys a hard time. If they had been, he would have had to knock heads. Gently of course, but still...

"Can I help you unpack anything?"

A.J. materialized out of the crowd. "Did I hear an offer of help? Even better, did I hear about food cooked by Mrs. Lyons? Where is she?"

"Mom and Dad already had plans to go sailing with their friends on the Bay today, otherwise they'd be here. Cullen put in an order for something sweet and fruity," Chelle explained. "Personally, I thought I was sweet, and Baily was fruity."

"Ha, ha...not." Cullen responded as he gathered Carys closer.

"Come on into the kitchen," A.J. motioned to the girls. "Carys, you better come now, the tarts will be gone before we even put them out on the table."

Baily put her arm through Carys', "Yeah, I want to hear how you're getting along with Aries."

"Not Cullen?" Carys asked as she started walking away.

"Nah, he's easy. Aries is the tough one," Cullen heard his sister saying just before the quartet were out of earshot.

As soon as they were gone, Zed Zaragoza sauntered over to him. He had been happily married for over a year and a half. He oozed contentment.

"You're just the man I wanted to talk to," Cullen said.

"And why would that be? Does it have anything to do with the good doctor? The way I hear it, you fell pretty hard while you were in Africa. Seems pretty unbelievable to me."

Cullen snorted. Thank God he hadn't taken a sip of his beer. Zed laughed.

"Did you really just say that?"

"We've started a club."

"Finding your woman on a mission and marrying her?"

"That's the one," Zed smirked. "Clint's next in line. He's finally got Lydia talked into setting a date."

"Did I hear that right?" Max Hogan said as he butted into the conversation. "Lydia and Clint Archer are finally going to tie the knot? How in the hell did Clint get her to say yes? It's only been four years."

"According to Marcia, it was praying over his bed day and night while he was in that coma. It tends to change your perspective," Zed answered.

"Is he really all right?" Kane entered the conversation.

"He's getting there," Zed sighed. "Goddamn injuries."

"Shut up, you asshole," Kane growled as he handed Zed some mineral water. "You almost fucking died. I don't want to hear you bitching about the fact that you get to spend time with your daughter."

Zed brightened up.

"Yeah, that little girl is growing by leaps and bounds."

"I'm going to see if I can go steal one of Mom's desserts before they're all gone," Cullen said as he clapped Zed on the back.

"Save one for me," Max called out as Cullen made his way to the kitchen.

"$\mathcal{I}$t must have been a hard decision to quit a vocation like Doctors Without Borders," Chelle said as she arranged the lemon tarts on a plate.

"Not that hard. I really think that job has a shelf-life. Your psyche can only take so much before you either crumple or become too hard and brittle to have the compassion needed to do a good job."

"Which do you think you would have done—the breaking, or the hard and brittle?" Baily asked.

Carys cocked her head as she looked at the youngest Lyons. She really was a blunt instrument.

"I don't know, Baily. I didn't stay long enough to find out."

"Which was pretty damn smart," A.J. said as she reached up to the top shelf for another serving plate. "Kane told me about the letters Cullen got from the family in Egypt," A.J. continued. "It must feel really good to know you could help like that."

"That case went well, unfortunately not every one does."

"Here, try this." Chelle handed Carys a napkin and a lemon tart. "Baily, stop being an ass."

"What? I want to make sure she's going to be good enough for Cullen. You know he's fallen hard for her."

Carys choked on her first bite and started coughing.

A.J. poured a glass of water and handed it to Carys as she took the dessert from her hand. She and Chelle glared at Baily.

"Let me rephrase that, little sister, don't be an asshole." Chelle said.

Carys' cough turned into a laugh. "Oh my God. Baily you're awesome. You're as protective as Cullen is."

"No, she's being a wench," Cullen said as he walked into the kitchen, put his arm around Carys' waist, and glared at his baby sister.

"Are you kidding me?" Carys beamed up at Cullen. "I would have given my right arm to have a family like this growing up. I can just imagine the amount of crud she gives you."

"Pardon me, but did you just say crud?" Baily asked.

"She doesn't swear," Cullen explained. "It's cute."

Baily laughed. "It is. You swear enough for two people, so it'll even out. You never told me, how do you get along with Aries?"

"He's a total traitor," Cullen answered. "I swear, in one day he has turned into Carys' dog."

Carys shook her head. "Don't you believe him. He's loyal to Cullen. He comes to him in an instant when he calls. But I've always wanted a pet."

The Lyons all looked at her. "You never had one?" Chelle asked. "Our house was a rescue center. Both kids and animals—that was thanks to Mom."

"Like I said, we grew up different."

"I'm kind of like you, Carys, no pets. I think we should compare notes," A.J. said as she plopped a tray into her hands. "Come on, let's get the table set up. The hoards are waiting." A.J. gave her a quick wink. She appreciated it. The woman knew that Carys didn't want to talk about how different her life had been from the normal household of the Lyons family.

Cullen blessed A.J. for her tact at the way she had deflected the conversation for Carys. He could have kicked his own ass. It was clear that his woman had felt uncomfortable about the difference in their upbringings. Maybe even a little melancholy. That was not what he wanted. But like normal, she'd bounced right back. Here she was in the middle of all his friends holding her own.

"I hear you and Python are now friends," Max smirked at Kane. "How does that work exactly?"

Kane grabbed both sides of his head and dropped it between his knees while he groaned. "Max, don't get me started. He gave us a cat."

"Be nice," A.J. swiped at him with the back of her hand. "You know Paul is a sweet soul," she said, referring to the aging eighties rock star.

"Honey, he's always going to be Old Sex Snake to

me. It's not my fault you decided to make him your business partner. What's more, I've been nice. We took the damn cat."

"Are you talking about that panther that is roaming around the house?" Leo snorted. "Scared the piss out of me."

"It's a Maine Coon, right?" Carys asked. "He's awfully friendly."

"What are you talking about?" Leo asked. "I thought I was going to be lunch."

"Carys is great with animals," Cullen said with pride. "How'd you know the breed?"

She shrugged her shoulders. As she did, the cat they were talking about jumped up into her lap with a thud. The big brown cat looked as big as Carys. He let out a yowl, then bumped his head against Carys' chin.

She laughed. "What's his name?"

"Big Bastard," Kane said under his breath.

"Viper," A.J. answered.

Carys wrapped her arms around the big cat and Leo stared in amazement. "Seriously, Carys, that cat hissed at me when he first saw me."

"You must have done something wrong. He's a love," Carys said as she scratched his jaw. Cullen started to get aroused. Kane saw and started to laugh. Now who was the big bastard?

"Hey, look who I found," Chelle said as she escorted Marcia Zaragoza to the back yard. Zed's wife was carrying her young daughter who immediately lit up when she saw Zed. She babbled something that sounded like 'Dada' and held out her arms for him, almost throwing herself out of her mother's arms.

"Let me get you a plate of food," A.J. offered as Zed got up and pulled out a seat at the picnic table for his wife to sit down next to him. He took his daughter who grinned happily up at her father.

Cullen glanced over at Carys who was still cuddling the cat and saw that she was watching the small family with avid interest. Yep, this was a woman who longed for the same things he did, even if she didn't quite know it yet. But that was his job, to get her to see that their futures were bound together. But after all he had said in Africa about his Dad falling for his Mom in one day, and Carys shutting down, he knew he needed to take it slow.

Damn, I want to tell her I love her and ask her to marry me. Tonight.

Down, Lyons! You're in it to win it. Don't rush.

Cullen sighed, and Carys looked over at him. "You all right?" she whispered.

"Perfect. Just don't think we're taking that cat home with us, Aries wouldn't like it."

She pulled back, "I would never assume to bring home a pet to your house. I know I'm just visiting, Cullen. But I really do appreciate how welcome you've made me."

It took a moment for him to be able to answer in a light tone. "Lady, I can't wait to welcome you some more tonight."

Her seductive laughter rang out into the night sky.

Soon, Lyons. Soon.

How in the heck had she become such a fixture at Cullen's house that she was planting pansies in his front yard? For that matter, how was it that she had gone to the garden center with Cullen's dad? Carys sat back on her knees and surveyed her handiwork. The flowers looked great bordering the walkway.

She was startled when a rope was dropped in front of her.

"You're as stealthy as your dad is," Carys laughed at Aries. "But I don't have time for tug-o-war today. I've got a couple of calls I have to make."

It was time to get back to reality. This extended vacation was coming to an end. No matter how much she would have liked it to last forever, she knew it couldn't. Cullen had been wonderful, but like fish, a guest starts to stink if they stick around too long.

She pushed away what Cullen had said last week about wanting her to stay in his arms forever. She figured that was just normal pillow-talk. It wasn't real.

Or was it?

Maybe she needed to sit him down and find out how he felt.

She got to her feet and snatched up the rope. Aries let out a yip of joy. She started to play an aggressive game with the dog, needing to get out some frustration. Darn-it-all, she wanted to stay. She *wanted* to stay in his arms forever, but he desired a family and the whole nine yards. But never once had he broached the subject with her. If he'd truly been interested in her, he would have at least talked to her about what she wanted in her future. But he hadn't.

"He doesn't want me, Aries," she muttered. She pulled really hard on the rope.

"You're being a wuss," she complained. "Fight."

~

Cullen drove up in time to see Carys and Aries really going at it in his front yard. It wasn't often that Aries fought as hard as he was doing in a game. He knew better than that. He stopped his Jeep at the bottom of his drive and got out. He would have whistled to get Aries to heel, but that would just land Carys on her ass. Hard.

"Aries, play nice," he shouted.

His dog immediately dialed it back. Carys didn't fall, but she did end up lurching back a few steps as she gained ground with the rope. She looked up at Cullen and glared. She dropped the rope.

"Not cool, Lyons. I wanted to win fair-and-square."

Nobody was due to come over, so Cullen left the Jeep where it was and sauntered up the drive. "The pansies look good," he smiled. "Not as good as you, but good."

"Stop with the sweet talk and tell me why you're home early. It's only four o'clock."

"I thought I'd take my best girl out on a picnic on the beach."

He saw her light up, but then she paused. "I really can't, I have a couple of phone calls I need to return."

He knew damn well what the phone calls were about. They were setting up job interviews across the country, and he'd be damned if he was going to let that happen.

"I have it all planned. Come on. It'll be fun. I promised Aries this morning before I left for work. Are you going to deny that face?" He looked over at his dog who gave the appropriate mournful expression.

Carys laughed. "How'd you get him to look at me like that? He looks pathetic."

"Trade secret. Now, are you going to come willingly, or do I have to carry you over my shoulder?"

She tapped her finger against her lip and gave him a considering look. "Willingly I suppose. But only for Aries, you understand."

"Of course."

"What do you need me to get?" she asked.

"You can change clothes. I figure you don't want to go to the beach all muddy."

She looked down at her dirty pedal pushers and frowned. "You're right. Give me just a minute, and I'll be right back. That should give you enough time to pack some sandwiches and put Aries in the Jeep."

"I'll be here," he promised.

As soon as she was in the house, he pulled out his phone.

"Baily?" he asked. "You got things under control?"

"She got away," his sister said.

"What do you mean she got loose?" Cullen couldn't believe it. Not now. This couldn't be happening. Not after all of his hard planning.

Chelle got onto the line. "Baily is screwing with you. Everything is under control. Just get Carys here, and everything will run like clockwork."

"Put Baily back on the phone," Cullen growled.

"No," Chelle answered. "First, because she's laughing too hard. Two, because you're just going to swear at her. Just get here. It's fine Cullen."

He hung up his phone and once again cursed having sisters. Well at least having a baby sister. Chelle was mostly okay, unless she was dating losers.

"Ready," Carys shouted out.

"Did you set the alarm?" Cullen asked as she came down the front steps.

Carys rolled her eyes. "Are you going to ask me that every time I leave the house?"

"How often do you ask me if I've washed my hands after I cook chicken?" he countered.

"Point taken. I set the alarm," she said as she smiled up at him.

"Let's go then. Something tells me this will be the best picnic of our lives."

Something was definitely strange. Carys didn't know what it was, but Cullen was acting anxious. Was he about to tell her that a mission was coming up and she needed to leave? No, that didn't sound right, if that were the case, he'd probably arrange for A.J., Chelle, Baily, Marcia and his mom to do rotations to come and visit her while he was away. Still, she could tell something was up, and it was making her stomach churn.

"Have you talked to Sarah lately?" he asked.

"Yep," she smiled. "Just last week. I thought I told you. The hospital where she works has a couple of vacancies."

"Yeah, you did tell me that," he said gruffly.

She shot him a startled glance. "I thought we agreed it would be good to get into a hospital where I could be around people I knew. As a matter of fact, that's exactly what you said."

"Hmm-hmm."

Carys leaned back in her seat. Yes, something was definitely off. Darn-it. She really wanted him to ask her to stay. Was that asking too much?

Is it time for me to man up? Or woman up?

"Cullen, there's something I want to say."

"Let's wait until we get to the beach."

"No seriously, there's something I need to get off my chest."

He turned to her, his eyes pleading. "Carys, we're almost there. Just a few more minutes, and then we can talk all you want about job offers, okay?"

"Fine."

She knew she was sounding petulant, but she couldn't help it.

When they made it to the beach parking lot, Cullen put the leash onto Aries. Once again he came around to open Carys' car door. It taken had a few weeks, but she finally learned to wait. Apparently, it was important to him, so she did it.

Okay, it was really kind of nice.

"Ready?" Cullen asked as he took her hand.

"Where's the food?" Carys asked as they started walking toward the beach.

"You'll see," he said mysteriously.

"You do have a way of keeping things interesting Mr. Lyons." Aries pulled at the leash, he was really excited to get to the water. They'd come to Chick Beach a couple of times before, and this was one of Aries' favorite places to play. If there weren't many people at the beach Cullen would let him loose and play fetch with him in the surf.

They came over the rise and she saw it was pretty much deserted except for a fire almost immediately in their line of sight. Beside it was blanket and a picnic basket. She looked up at Cullen and back at the set-up then back at Cullen. "Is that ours?"

"Damn right."

"You're good."

He squeezed her hand as they made their way down to the blanket. She knelt down and looked at the plates all set up. Then she spied a bucket of ice with a bottle in it. She pulled it out.

"Champagne?"

"Dig deeper."

She looked farther in the bucket, and grinned. There was a can of pineapple Fanta. "I wasn't sure which you would prefer," he said.

She leaned back on her knees and looked at the man she loved, as she held the bottle of champagne in one hand and the can of Fanta in the other. They were both wet and dripping on her jeans. "What's going on?"

"Just one more minute, Beautiful."

He let out a long whistle. Aries perked up.

"Not you," he gave Aries the hand signal to sit. He sat down with his tongue hanging out. But then he stood up again, which was totally unlike him after getting a command. He barked once. A dog came bounding over the sand toward their blanket. It was beautiful. Carys couldn't tell if it was a Malamute or a Husky.

"Good girl," Cullen said as she skidded to a stop before the blanket.

"Come here, Betsey." The dog daintily walked onto the blanket toward Cullen and put her face down onto her front paws.

"Oh my God, what a love," Carys exclaimed.

"She's a rescue. She needs a home. I thought you might like to be her owner." For the first time since she'd known him, Cullen sounded less than confident.

"You want me to take care of Betsey? But I don't even know where I'm going to end up living."

"Check out her collar," Cullen whispered.

With a trembling hand, Carys scratched Betsey's head as she looked up at her with soulful blue eyes, reminding her of Cullen. Then Betsey put her head in Carys' lap. Carys looked at the collar and saw it was engraved with Cullen's address.

When she looked up at Cullen, he was holding a ring.

"I love you so much Carys. I think I've loved you

from the moment I laid eyes on you. Definitely since that night in the truck underneath the stars. Will you be my wife, have fun with me, and fill my house with dogs, cats and children and live with me forever?"

It was her every dream come true.

"Oh Cullen, I've loved you forever too, but I fell in love with you the night you held me at David and Sarah's house. I would have lost my soul if I had to leave you," she choked out.

"That's never going to happen. There wasn't a chance in hell you were going to get away from me," Cullen said as he pulled her left hand toward him and slid the antique diamond ring onto her finger.

In the background she heard the barks of the dogs as they played in the surf, but that was soon drowned out by his kiss. His kiss, that went on and on.

She was home.

EPILOGUE

"*M*ore mail for you, and it damn well better not be another job offer from out of state," Cullen said grumpily. It was one of their rare Saturdays where they had no plans, and he had just come in from mowing the front yard.

"What are you worried about," Carys asked as she caressed Cullen's cheek. "I've got three job offers in Virginia Beach."

"I hated the one you got from Cedar-Sinai in California. That was pretty damn prestigious, even *I* thought you should take it."

Carys laughed. "Are you kidding? I would have been working eighty hours a week and your commute to Coronado would have been hellish. That is not the life I wanted to live." She loved her man. These rare moments of insecurity always took her by surprise.

"Come on, let's go into our office and shred any job offers, then go take a nap."

His grin was huge. "I like the sound of a nap."

So, did she. She *loved* napping with Cullen, he was always so inventive.

"Has mom called?" Cullen asked with an evil gleam in his eye as they headed to the office.

"You should have told me she had a wedding file for your sisters. My God Cullen, not in my wildest dreams did I ever think that someone could be so excited about planning a wedding."

He pulled her to a stop in the hallway and backed her up against the wall. "Are you okay with it? I can tell her to back off."

Carys smiled. She thought about her own mother who had barely had any reaction at all after she determined Carys was marrying a 'soldier'. As far as Carys was concerned her parents could count themselves lucky if they got an invitation to the wedding. Heck, she might have Rosa walk her down the aisle.

"What are you grinning about?" Cullen asked, his gaze piercing.

"Nothing."

"It's not nothing."

"Seriously, it is. Did you know how lucky I am to have you? To have your family? I love you Mr. Lyons."

"I love you, soon-to-be Mrs. Dr. Lyons."

Carys grinned. "Let's go shred, so we can nap."

She pushed at his chest and they moved to the office.

She sorted through the mail on the way to the office and as she got to the desk, Cullen reached for her.

"Let's start the nap in here," he breathed into her hair.

She turned into his arms. His mouth met hers. It was just a light brush of his lips. A small temptation of what was to come. She reached up and attempted to pull his head down. He smiled, and she relished his tease. Two could play this game. She bit his neck, then laved it with her tongue, loving the low growl that came from deep inside his chest.

He backed her up against the desk and lifted her up on it. One of the envelopes fluttered to the floor.

"Wait a minute," she pushed against him.

"What?"

"It's from Clint and Lydia."

"What is?" he dropped another kiss against her jaw.

"Pick it up."

He gave a put-upon sigh and bent down and picked it up. Then grinned widely. "Whoo Hoo, looks like my man is finally doing the big deed." Cullen tore open the envelope. "Yep, here it is. A wedding invitation. They're getting married at Jack and Beth's ranch in Texas."

"Before or after us?" Carys asked.

"Before." He threw the invitation on the desk. "Now, where was I? Oh yeah, I remember. I was about to pick up my woman and take her for a nap."

He pulled Carys into his arms and kissed her right this time. No teasing, just a kiss to end all kisses, and Carys knew she was loved.

∽

Thank you for reading *Her Tempting Protector*, I hope you enjoyed it. For all the latest Night Storm news subscribe to my newsletter. Subscribe Here.

ABOUT THE AUTHOR

USA Today Bestselling Author, Caitlyn O'Leary, adores writing Military Romantic Suspense and Paranormal Romance. She started publishing books in 2014. Storytelling has been a tradition in her family for years, and she still holds on to the letters she has received from family members since her childhood.

Caitlyn lives in California with her husband John of sixteen years who often makes guest appearances in her reader group, Caitlyn's Crew. Getting to know so many people within the reader community is almost as much fun as writing each new novel. So join her reader group so she can get to know you, and see if she and John can make it to year seventeen!

You never know what kind of book she'll write next, it all depends on what strikes her fancy. Be sure to keep in touch.

Keep up with Caitlyn O'Leary:

Website: www.caitlynoleary.com
Email: caitlyn@caitlynoleary.com
Newsletter: http://caitlynoleary.com/newsletter/

facebook.com/Caitlyn-OLeary-Author-638771522866740

twitter.com/CaitlynOLearyNA

instagram.com/caitlynoleary_author

amazon.com/author/caitlynoleary

bookbub.com/authors/caitlyn-o-leary

goodreads.com/CaitlynOLeary

pinterest.com/caitlynoleary35

ALSO BY CAITLYN O'LEARY

NIGHT STORM SERIES

Her Ruthless Protector (Book #1)

Her Tempting Protector (Book #2)

THE MIDNIGHT DELTA SERIES

Her Vigilant Seal (Book #1)

Her Loyal Seal (Book #2)

Her Adoring Seal (Book #3)

Seal with a Kiss (Book #4)

Her Daring Seal (Book #5)

Her Fierce Seal (Book #6)

A Seals Vigilant Heart (Book #7)

Her Dominant Seal (Book #8)

Her Relentless Seal (Book #9)

Her Treasured Seal (Book #10)

BLACK DAWN SERIES

Her Steadfast Hero (Book #1)

Her Devoted Hero (Book #2)

Her Passionate Hero (Book #3)

Her Wicked Hero (Book #4)

Her Guarded Hero (Book #5)

Her Captivated Hero (Book #6)

Her Honorable Hero (Book #7)

Her Loving Hero (Book #8)

THE FOUND SERIES

Revealed (Book #1)

Forsaken (Book #2)

Healed (Book #3)

SHADOWS ALLIANCE SERIES

Declan

FATE HARBOR SERIES

Trusting Chance (Book #1)

Protecting Olivia (Book #2)

Claiming Kara (Book #3)

Isabella's Submission (Book #4)

Cherishing Brianna (Book #5)

Made in the USA
Las Vegas, NV
20 January 2024

84532190R00157